He was a delicious specimen

Dark hair flowed to the nape of his neck; black brows scowled over denim-blue eyes that seemed confused yet missed nothing.

He was a good six foot four to her five-four, yet he moved gracefully, even holding a baby. She could only hope he looked as good when he took off his costume.

What was it about her and bad boys, the rougher/tougher, the better? She'd snatched him before any other "lady" in the show could— never let it be said that Auburn McGinnis ran from *all* men. Just the *last* man. And she planned to keep running, with this baby and her handsome daddy, if her lucky stars were out tonight.

Dear Reader,

I do love writing Christmas stories, and this one is my favorite yet. What fun to write about a man and a woman who find each other through impossible odds and different centuries!

I've often wondered what it would be like to experience a different time and place, so getting to put myself into the lives of a hero and heroine in nineteenth-century Texas was a thrilling adventure. I'm a big believer in angels, ghosts and blessings that get passed down through time, so living in Christmas River with Dillinger and Auburn—and Rose and Polly—gave me a special sense of hope and affirmation that the ones we love are always very much with us.

I hope you enjoy *The Cowboy from Christmas Past*, and spending the holiday season in Christmas River. Blessings to you all at this wonderful, miraculous time of year!

Always much love,

Tina Leonard

Tina Leonard

THE COWBOY FROM CHRISTMAS PAST

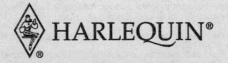

TORONTO • NEW YORK • LONDON
AMSTERDAM • PARIS • SYDNEY • HAMBURG
STOCKHOLM • ATHENS • TOKYO • MILAN • MADRID
PRAGUE • WARSAW • BUDAPEST • AUCKLAND

Recycling programs
for this product may
not exist in your area.

ISBN-13: 978-0-373-75286-7

THE COWBOY FROM CHRISTMAS PAST

www.eHarlequin.com

Printed in U.S.A.

ABOUT THE AUTHOR

Tina Leonard is a bestselling author of more than forty projects, including a popular thirteen-book miniseries for Harlequin American Romance. Her books have made the Waldenbooks, Ingram's and Nielsen BookScan bestseller lists. Tina feels she has been blessed with a fertile imagination and quick typing skills, excellent editors and a family who loves her career. Born on a military base, she lived in many states before eventually marrying the boy who did her crayon printing for her in the first grade. Tina believes happy endings are a wonderful part of a good life. You can visit her at www.tinaleonard.com.

Books by Tina Leonard

Special thanks to Anne Stuart—
brainstorming this idea with you was so much fun!
Many thanks to the members of the Tina Leonard's
Nightstand newsletter for being so enthusiastic
about this story, and also to Georgia Haynes for
editing. Much, much gratitude goes to the very
loyal readers who graciously and faithfully support
my career. And as always, Lisa, Dean and Tim—
you are the love behind my writing.

Chapter One

*Somewhere in the Texas Panhandle, Christmas
season of 1892*

For Dillinger Kent, retired gunslinger, life was quiet on
his thousand-acre spread on the outskirts of the Texas
Panhandle town of Christmas River. Winter with its
promise of bitter cold and occasional snow, unlike the
rest of the state, made his solitary lifestyle even more
remote. Springtime brought fullness to his ranch, with
trees and grasses dressing the stark landscape in
glorious greens; summer and fall brought their own
lustrous hues to warm the countryside.

But the Christmas season was a harbinger of the icy
cocoon soon to envelop him for the next three months. It
was the middle of December, and deep winter crept closer.

He'd chosen a life of loneliness when he'd lost his
wife, Polly Hartskill Kent. They'd made plans for a

family out here, a big home to raise them in. Christmas on the ranch, Polly said, would be so much fun with lots of little feet running around. Polly had a beautiful soul and Dillinger had loved her as he would never love anyone again. But his darling wife had taken ill with pneumonia during the last Christmas season, and having a beautiful soul hadn't saved her.

He picked up a self-portrait Polly had drawn for him, which he'd put in a wooden frame. She was luminous, even in charcoal. Her kindness and grace of spirit was captured in the lines of her likeness. He set the picture down and picked up a pair of small, dangling earrings with tiny golden bells. They were delicate, like Polly. He'd given them to her two Christmases ago, a wedding gift he'd picked up on his last trip to California. She'd been thrilled with them, giggling when they lightly tinkled at her ears. The earrings felt like a tiny memory between his rough fingers. He would never give them to another woman, would never part with them.

Dillinger forced his mind away from Polly. He wondered if he might go crazy one day in this isolated countryside. But he knew it was just the date on the calendar he'd bought at Gin's Feed Store that was making him maudlin. He'd make it to springtime—he swore that he would. He curled his fingers around the earrings, then set them back on the desk, barely able to turn them loose.

The wind whipped around outside the nine-room home he'd built with his own hands. No chill would seep in—he knew every inch of his house and it was tight against the elements. Dillinger closed his eyes, wondered if he should go check the livestock, which would be huddled in close groups for warmth. They were more than likely fine.

Still, he had the urge to look outside.

Then he heard the wailing.

It came thin at first, carried by the wind. It wasn't an animal's cry—it sounded human. But at this time of night, nearly ten o'clock, there would be no people around. His ranch was far from town, hardly a convenient place for someone to stop by.

Yet he heard it again. He buttoned his long oilskin coat, which reached below his knees. Grabbing gloves and setting his cowboy hat tight on his head, he prepared for the gusts of wind that would tear at him. He stepped out and nearly onto a basket that had been laid on his porch. By God, it was a baby, a pink-wrapped thing in a wicker basket.

Dillinger looked in all directions, but there were no footprints in the snow leading away from the house. Yet the baby couldn't have been there long. "Hey!" he called into the darkness. "You can't leave this here! Come back!"

The poor woman who had left her child here didn't

understand. He lived alone. He went to town only four times a year. He was basically a pariah.

The gossip mill of Christmas River had turned on him after Polly's death, and to his shock, it was said that Polly had died of pneumonia after trying to flee from him one cold December night. Her parents had claimed that he was jealous, had become aware that another man wanted to court Polly, and that Dillinger had chased her down, intending to murder her in cold blood.

Now he was a man with no town.

"Come back here!" he yelled into the breath-stealing chill of the snowstorm. But there was no answer, just the cries of the desperate baby at his feet.

So he picked up the basket, cursing it, cursing himself, his life…and found himself in a shootout straight from the Old West. Three gunslingers he'd never seen before aimed pistols at him. Gaudily attired saloon women screamed and ran for cover. With his holster and gun missing, he had no choice but to do what he could to save the baby in his arms.

He jumped off the stage and into a seated throng of clapping women, men and children. Popcorn flew, but there was no time to apologize; he expected a bullet in his back any second. Somehow he had to get the baby to shelter. He ran to the nearest safe place he could find—a theater box with a sign on it that read Security, empty for the moment—and looked down at the baby.

Dillinger's chest heaved, but the infant looked up at him, calm now and gazing at him reverently.

"Hey." A saloon woman squeezed into the box with him. "You're going to be in big trouble with Harry."

He stared at his unwanted companion. Her long, whiskey-colored hair fell in cascading curls, her green eyes huge.

"Harry?"

"Yeah. He's not going to be happy that you rewrote the script. Nor that you had a baby onstage."

Dillinger held the infant closer.

"Couldn't you find a sitter?" she asked. "I know it's late at night, but surely a teenager would have been willing to watch your baby."

He couldn't speak, his world changing so fast he couldn't take it in. He felt himself shift into survival mode. He studied the woman's painted lips—a sweet, shiny cherry—and her long, long lashes. He'd never seen a woman wear so much face paint and yet have so little need of it.

Whoever she was—whatever she was—he needed her right now.

She shook her head. "I've only been here a few weeks and you're clearly real new, but if I were you, I'd go to Harry after the act is over, apologize like hell and beg him not to fire you. Six Flags is crawling with people looking for work, even at Christmastime."

Dillinger frowned. "I wouldn't beg for anything. And what do you mean, when the act is over?"

"That was the last scene, the grand finale." She shrugged pale, softly rounded shoulders. "Suit yourself on the begging part, but you can't perform with the baby." She cast a glance over him. "You may look like the real McCoy, but Harry's not going to bend rules even for you, I bet."

The infant began to cry, a wail that suggested she was hungry and didn't care to wait. "I'm not in an act. I'm lost," he said, and the saloon dancer laughed.

"No kidding, cowboy," she said. "You're just one egg shy of a dozen, aren't you?"

"I need help."

He watched, fascinated, as she pulled a black mole off the skin above her gently curved lips. "Let's get out of here. I need to wash my face, and we'll figure out where to find baby formula and Pampers. Unless you're going to surprise me and say you've got some in your car."

He shook his head, not certain what she had just asked him. She sighed and motioned for him to follow her from the box.

"What about Harry?" He presumed Harry employed her, but maybe there was more to it than that.

"To hell with him," she said, "we need to feed Princess Squall. I feel sorry for her." She smiled down at the baby and her face softened. "Thank God I never had one of these or I might not have ever had the courage to back out of my wedding at the last minute. You're a sweetie," she said, lifting the baby from his arms. "You should have gummed on Daddy's nose for forgetting your bottle, honey."

He watched protectively as she cuddled the infant. The baby stopped crying and Dillinger relaxed slightly.

He needed one person on his side right now. As much as he might not like it, the saloon dancer would have to do, at least until he figured out exactly how the hell he'd gotten here.

OKAY, THE GUNSLINGER WAS an odd bird and she didn't need drama right now—staying in hiding would be harder with a baby—but he seemed harmless, and if nothing else, at least not a perv. He hadn't so much as glanced at her low-cut gown—the gaudy yellow polyester thing—so she could do worse than odd.

At the moment, she couldn't really be picky about who she hung around with. In spite of her tough words, this was her last night in the show. She'd been here a month; it was time to move on if she wanted to stay ahead of her ex-fiancé. After she'd left Bradley in New York City, she'd developed an itch to keep putting distance between them.

She carried the baby like a treasured artifact through the crowds, leaving the man to follow, as she knew he would. The tall, dark, handsome stranger hadn't wanted to part with the baby, but like any wise female, she employed the carrot-and-stick approach when necessary. The baby was the carrot, and the cowboy stayed glued to her heels.

He was a delicious, if silent, specimen. Dark hair flowed to the nape of his neck; black brows scowled over denim-blue eyes that seemed confused, yet missed nothing. He was a good six feet four, a foot taller than her, yet he moved gracefully, even when running with a baby. She could only hope he looked as good when he took off his costume. What was it about her and bad boys, the rougher and tougher, the better? She'd snatched him before any other "lady" in the show could—never let it be said that Auburn McGinnis ran from *all* men. Just the *last* man. And she planned to keep running, with this baby and her handsome daddy, if her lucky stars were out tonight.

They didn't speak much in the car. He seemed preoccupied and Auburn was relieved when she pulled into the penthouse parking lot twenty minutes later. They'd purchased diapers, formula and sundry baby things, since the cowboy seemed to have nothing with him. She was a tad suspicious that he'd snatched the baby from its mother, but kept her thoughts to herself. He'd flee if he suspected she was going to call the police, and the best thing to do would be to protect the baby. She could watch the news tonight and see if there was an Amber Alert. She'd cast a quick eye at the lighted overhead sign as they'd driven along the highway, which flashed with a description when a child had been stolen.

There'd been no warning.

"What's your name?" Auburn asked.

The cowboy had been turned around in his seat, staring at the baby in the back, almost as if reassuring himself that she was there. "My name?"

"Yes." Auburn sighed. "You can relax. She's not going to disappear."

Her words seemed to agitate him and he once again stared back at the newly purchased car seat containing the baby. He was edgy, and it began to occur to Auburn that she had to be an idiot for picking up a man who had no car—claimed he didn't—no diapers or food for a baby— bad sign—and had a major possessive streak going on.

"You're not that child's daddy," she said, blurting out her thoughts as she turned off the car.

To her shock, he didn't look as if he was about to grab the baby and dash off.

"I know," he said. "She was given to me."

"People don't give away babies."

"Trust me, I tried to give her back."

Auburn considered that as she got out of the car. "Be careful when you take her out. Remove the entire carrier and bring it inside. I don't have a crib, but she can sleep in her carrier if she's comfortable, at least for the time being. We can make her a nice, soft pallet on the floor if we need to."

Auburn watched as he picked up the carrier, handling it as if the baby were gold. A deep breath escaped her. Maybe he was telling the truth; most single men probably wouldn't be thrilled to have a baby thrust upon them. And he didn't look exactly scary. If anything, he was eye candy, the kind of man women would jump all over to have his child.

Unlocking the door to her apartment, Auburn said, "Back to your name."

"Dillinger Kent." He waited beside her, curious as she opened the door. "What kind of place is this?"

"My name's Auburn McGinnis," she said calmly, closing the door behind them, "and this is called a penthouse. Is that what you're asking?"

He seemed overwhelmed. "I don't know," he said, sounding tired as he carefully set the baby down. "Have you ever had a dream that felt like it was real?"

She eyed him suspiciously. "I'm going to get out of this costume. Make yourself at home. There's a powder room down the hall."

"Powder room?"

Maybe his family called them something else. "A place to freshen up."

He nodded, saying nothing more as he sank onto the

sofa, his gaze riveted on the baby once again. She slept peacefully in her car seat carrier, oblivious to any change in her fortunes.

Auburn went to take off her stage makeup, and when she returned, the cowboy was sound asleep on her sofa, sitting up. He was truly delicious. If a woman liked her men hot, protective and dark-haired, this one had all the right stuff.

He also might be a baby thief. She ignored her sudden awareness of how wonderfully chiseled his features were, locked her bedroom door and went to bed. In the morning, she'd figure out what to do about the cowboy, and the baby.

Auburn awakened, aware of someone in the bedroom with her. She blinked tired eyes, coming straight awake as she realized the cowboy was beside her bed. "Eee!" she shrieked, jumping out from under the sheet and flipping on the light. "What are you doing in here?"

He seemed as startled as she was. "I just came to tell you that the baby wants something."

Auburn clutched her nightshirt close to her. "How did you get in here?" She was positive she'd locked the door. It was locked now. She turned frightened eyes on the handsome stranger.

"I walked in." He looked at her strangely. "I'm sorry. I should have knocked."

"Yes, you should have!" Auburn glared at him. "And why are you telling me that the baby wants something?"

"Because I don't know what she wants!" he snapped. "I've never had a baby before!"

Auburn opened the door and swept past him to pick up the child. "How long have you had her?"

"Just a few minutes before I met you. I think."

She took the baby from the carrier, handing her to Dillinger, who seemed as surprised as the child. She quit crying for the moment. "Look," Auburn said over her shoulder as she went to prepare a bottle, "when the baby cries, she wants to be fed, probably about every three hours or so. She'll want her diaper changed, and you'll be in charge of that. Then she'll want to be cuddled and burped, and you'll be in charge of that, too." She handed him the bottle. "I'm not in charge of any of this. It's not my baby."

"Mine, either, but I like her." He took the bottle, cradled the baby and sat down on the sofa.

Amber watched, curious. She knew something about the care of children, certainly. She'd volunteered in the church nursery; her family often had toddlers running around from different branches of the family. But this cowboy didn't seem that well versed in holding a baby or feeding one, because it took him a few seconds to get the bottle just right so that the little one settled down enough to drink.

He wasn't making it up, Auburn realized. This wasn't his baby, and there were no Amber Alerts on the news last night. "Who gave her to you?" she asked softly.

"I don't know. She was left on my porch. Which was a strange thing to do, because it had to be all of twenty degrees outside."

It was fifty-five in Dallas. Auburn shook her head. "Where do you live?"

"Christmas River."

"Texas?"

He looked at her. "Yes."

She pulled her iPhone from her purse, searching the Internet for the town. A chill swept over. Nothing. It didn't exist. "There's no such place."

He shook his head at her. "Of course there is. I have a ranch there."

"Is there a nickname the town goes by?"

"It's Christmas River," he insisted.

She looked up the name Dillinger Kent, Christmas River. Her heart felt like it completely stopped. On a Web site of a Texas historical society there was a reprint of what looked like an old newspaper article.

Notorious gunslinger Dillinger Kent shot and killed one of the most infamous stagecoach robbers of all time, Harmon Keith, outside of Carson City today.

The date on the article was May 16, 1888. "What's your real name?"

The baby stopped sucking on the bottle for an instant, then resumed. Dillinger looked at her. "I told you."

"No, you gave me a name of a gunslinger from the 1880s." There were no other Dillinger Kents listed, though she could check Facebook next. She tapped the Web address in quickly. Nothing.

"I was a gunslinger," he said, "but I gave it up when I took a wife."

Great. He was married. Auburn should have known. The whole story was bogus. He'd had some kind of spat with his wife, snatched the baby and took off.

Auburn backed into the bedroom doorway. This was a complication she totally didn't need.

Chapter Two

Dillinger was worried. Something was badly wrong. Either he was having a terrible dream or...well, he didn't know what else this could be. But something wasn't good. One minute he'd picked a baby up off his porch, and the next thing he knew, he was in another century. And when he'd woken up to the baby's cries and wondered how to soothe her, Auburn's name had popped into his mind—although she didn't seem like the type who would know a whole lot about babies—and he'd found himself inside her bedroom.

Just like that.

Right now she was staring at him with an expression of distrust and maybe even regret, for which he couldn't blame her. No woman of decent family took a man into her home—a man with whom she wasn't acquainted—and then was happy he'd materialized in her bedroom.

They were on bad footing here. She didn't like him, and he needed her.

He had to convince her to help him.

"You're married," she said flatly. "Did you kidnap that baby from your wife? Did you have an argument?"

"No. My wife is dead." He looked to see some sympathy in her expression, but if anything, Auburn appeared even more horrified. She had the same expression on her face that the people of Christmas River wore when they saw him, as if he were no better than a common murderer.

While he might have been known to gun down a man, he had never treated a woman with anything but respect. And he'd handled his beloved Polly as if she were a china doll. "I didn't kill my wife," he said dully.

"I didn't say you did."

"You didn't have to," he muttered. The baby in his arms hesitated again, searching his face for a few moments before continuing with her peaceful feeding. Something about the little one calmed him, made him feel a connection he couldn't quite understand and yet welcomed. This baby had brought him here. "You and me," he told the child, "we're sticking together."

He heard a sigh and glanced back up at the woman framed in her bedroom doorway. She was prettier without cosmetic artifice. He guessed she had to wear it for the theater production in which she performed—another bad sign, of course. Women who made their living on the stage weren't in the same class as women who married and kept a home for a husband. But as a gunslinger, he'd lived far outside the norms of convention, too.

Still, he wished a woman of high standards had found him, for the sake of the baby. The woman wore a long T-shirt that read I'm Shakespeare's Girl, which wasn't possible because Shakespeare had lived and died in a previous time, the sixteenth and seventeenth centuries. If she were, in fact, acquainted with Shakespeare in some way, she'd have to be able to travel through time like a ghost, which simply wasn't possible.

At least he hadn't thought it was.

"What are you going to do with that baby? And what's her name?"

It hadn't occurred to him that the warm bundle needed a name other than The Baby, which was how he thought of her. He studied her round face, big, blue eyes, sweet button nose. "Her name is Rose," he said quickly, "and she is my…my daughter." He glared at Auburn. "I will protect her and raise her as if she's my very own."

Auburn shook her head. "You have to turn her in to the authorities."

Oh, he knew all about the authorities. There'd be no fair shake for him and Rose with them. "Just let me sleep with her on this divan," he said, "and I'll be on my way tomorrow."

"That's fine. I need to be moving on myself. However, just a warning, Dillinger," she said. "The next woman you meet is going to ask the same questions I have. Eventually, you'll be caught."

He laughed. He couldn't help himself. Rose finished her bottle, so he lifted her up to his chest. She gave a satisfying, unladylike belch, which also made him laugh. "Wouldn't that be rich? Hanged because I'm guarding a child?"

"Hanged?" Auburn frowned. "Isn't that a little dramatic?"

He didn't know. "I'm tired," he finally said. Tired of being tempted by long legs and immodest thoughts about a woman who wasn't his wife. "Rose and I thank you for your hospitality, and your help. We won't trouble you past the morning."

"Fine, bud. Whatever you say." She yawned and grasped the doorknob. "I'd turn you in to the police, but I don't want to be found right now myself. You seem like you have that baby's best interests at heart, and enough money to take care of her, so I'm not going to ask any more questions. All I ask is that you don't come into my room again. Okay? If you need something, you can give a shout, but no more of the lock trick. It's kind of stalkerish."

It was his turn to frown. "You're not my type," he said. "You need have no fear of anything untoward from me."

She looked at him. "Glad we understand each other."

They didn't, but it wasn't important. "Good night," he said, and busied himself changing Rose's diaper. It was going to be a struggle, but he'd watched Auburn change one, and the plastic tapes didn't seem as challenging as firing a gun at a moving target. Rose wiggled and he taped her leg, so he had to start over. He tried not to fumble under Auburn's scrutiny—he could tell the whiskey-haired woman didn't completely trust him with the baby.

And then he felt the strangest sensation run through him, like cold on a hot summer day, and a tingling that ran all over him in the worst kind of way—as if a ghost had just walked over his grave.

He hated Dillinger Kent. He was going to kill the gunslinger the second he tracked his murdering carcass down. Pierre Hartskill stood in the ranch house where Dillinger lived, eyeing the place where his sister had been trapped in a loveless marriage. A few logs in the fireplace were charred, the embers below still gray and smoldering as if Dillinger had left in a hurry. Maybe he knew Pierre was on his way to kill him. Perhaps a black angel guarded Dillinger from reaping his just desserts, forewarning him of his impending death. Pierre wasn't afraid of the reputed gunslinger. Fear was not an option, nor was mercy.

He was going to run him down as Dillinger had Polly,

and then he was going to put a bullet through him. And no angel was going to save him.

On the writing desk lay a golden earring. Pierre recognized it. Polly had worn them often, loving the feel of the tiny bells as they danced against her skin. He picked the earring up with cold-chapped fingers, and gave it a shake to hear the bells tinkle again.

And from somewhere faraway, yet loud enough to seem as if it came from this very room, Pierre heard a man cry out.

AUBURN GASPED AS THE COWBOY let out a yell of surprise and suddenly went airborne. Thank heaven he'd put the baby on her pallet! He tossed around violently in the air before landing on the couch. He lay still, gasping for breath, crumpled in his long duster, his boots hanging over the edge of the sofa.

"Are you all right?" Auburn wasn't sure if she should touch him or stay far away. Dillinger was a funny color, his face ashen, as if he might be sick any second. She'd be sick if she'd gotten tossed around like that—she didn't even like to ride the superdizzying rides at Six Flags.

"I'm fine," he groaned.

"You're not fine! What the heck did you just do?" He seemed too sick to harm her, so she approached him, peering down at his prone body.

"A lady doesn't swear," he said, groaning again.

"And a man doesn't fly around a room. I suggest you explain that particular magic trick before I decide to call the law on you, buddy," she said sternly. "And don't you dare tell me not to swear!"

He tried to sit up, but failed. "No law. Please."

Well, she wouldn't call the law on him—not yet—but she didn't want him doing that weird levitation again. "Hey, do you want a drink of water?"

"Just take care of the baby," he said quietly. And then passed out.

"Of all the nerve!" Auburn stared at both of them, sleeping like, well, babies, and a little pity slid into her heart. The man was too big to sleep on the tiny rental furniture, and he was pretty tangled up in that duster. He couldn't be comfortable. Carefully, she tugged his legs off the sofa so that he was on his back, hanging over one edge, sure, but at least he wasn't in a ball any longer. "You're weird," she told him, but he didn't move. So she dragged the blanket and comforter off her bed and settled down on the floor beside the sofa next to the baby. "You have a scary daddy," she told Rose, but the funny thing was, Auburn wasn't really afraid of Dillinger anymore.

She was afraid *for* him.

THIRTY MINUTES LATER THE sound of knocking startled Auburn awake. If she hadn't been deeply asleep, she might have thought twice about opening the door, but she was operating on autopilot. She woke up in a hurry when the security guard peered at her.

"You left your car lights on," he said. "Thought you might want to know." His gaze widened as he caught sight of the cowboy on her sofa and the baby on the floor.

"Yes, thank you," Auburn said, hastily trying to close the door. "I'll take care of it right now."

He was mentally cataloging the strange scene in her living room. This was trouble, since she didn't want any details left behind for an ex-fiancé, who surely had people looking for her. "Thank you," she said again, more curtly this time, and closed the door.

Locking it, she took a deep breath. Closed her eyes. Wondered why simply running out on a bad idea like a wedding had to be so worrying. She should never have said yes in the first place, should never have allowed her parents to make her feel that she had to find her Prince Charming.

"What are you afraid of?" Dillinger asked, and Auburn jumped.

"I'm not afraid of anything," she said, grabbing her keys from her purse. "What makes you say such a silly thing?"

He sat up, shrugged. "Just seems that I'm not the only one with secrets."

"No, but you are the only one who can make himself spin around in the air."

He frowned. "What do you mean?"

She gazed at him. "Don't you remember?"

"Remember what?"

She circled a finger in the air. "Your levitation trick."

He gave her a strange look, as if he figured she was crazy. "I've been asleep on the sofa."

He didn't remember. Chills ran over Auburn's skin. Yet she hadn't imagined it. "I'm going to go turn off my car lights. Then you and I should probably talk."

Shrugging again, he pulled his hat low over his face. She took that as a masculine sign of agreement and left to turn off the car lights before her battery died. A dead car was the last thing she needed, because she had a prickly sensation that it was time to hit the road.

The only question left was whether she took companions with her or left them to their own confused journey.

She wasn't sure she could do that to little Rose.

Chapter Three

Dillinger watched the woman walk out the door to go fix her automobile—or so she said. He wasn't sure what the petite fireball was up to—maybe she thought she could make him think he was insane with that weird conversation about him flying around—but a woman like that begged for caution. Her quick, soft conversation with the man who'd come to the door worried him, and he hadn't missed the gleam in her eyes when she glanced at Rose. If there was ever a lady looking for a baby, Auburn was it. It showed in her concern, and her careful handling and her distrust of him. He wouldn't trust him, either, baby or not—but he could feel her longing for the infant like a man longed for peace and quiet. And she was on the run, another reason he didn't trust her. Everybody had something to hide—he did, too—but a woman who was used to running might just decide to run with his precious bundle.

He'd looked into the eyes of thieves many a time. They carried a hungry, focused, almost desperate aura, all the while trying to fool you with their calm. He was in a strange place, with things he didn't recognize all around him. All he knew was that he had to protect the one thing he had with him, which seemed to have brought him here, if he ever hoped to get back home again, home to his ranch and to the memories of Polly. Carefully, he wrapped up Rose's things in a sack he found in Auburn's kitchen, snuggled the baby in his arms and slipped out the door.

"Hey!"

He heard Auburn's sweet-toned voice, tinged with some anxiety. She was at the elevator, not gone long enough to get to her car.

"What are you doing?" she demanded.

"Leaving," he said, deciding one of them had to be honest. "We're in your way."

"Not more than anything else," Auburn said. "Please don't go."

That shocked him. He'd expected a protest from her, but not a gentle request. "We need to."

"You don't even know where you're going, do you?"

He didn't. Why admit it? "Rose and I will do fine."

"I don't understand," she said, and he hardened his heart.

"You don't really need to. We only just met you. You're not our problem. I mean, we're not your problem."

She cocked her head. "You're not a problem, really. Something's wrong."

The confusion in her pretty eyes was very alluring. When she wasn't dolled up, and when she showed her soft side like this, she was quite fetching. She might not have Polly's innocent beauty, but was enticing nonetheless. Dillinger didn't let himself recognize the sudden stab of unwelcome attraction he felt for the woman.

"It's better this way." He wanted to walk past her to the elevator, to get away before Rose awakened and needed another bottle, but part of him seemed stuck to the floor.

"Hey," Auburn said, her voice soft, "I really need you."

His brows raised of their own accord. "Why?"

She seemed to choose her words carefully. "Protection."

She'd already had one man visit her abode, the so-called security guard. She'd run with Dillinger from a boss named Harry. The kind of protection she needed didn't seem to require further description. "I— No. I'm not for hire."

She stepped closer. He could smell her fresh-washed scent, look into her pleading eyes. Automatically, he shut off the part of him that wanted to ask what protection she could possibly need.

"I need help," she said, "and a hired gun is just what I need."

He narrowed his gaze. "You didn't believe me earlier when I told you who I was."

She shook her head. "I don't know what to believe about you."

"The sentiment is mutual."

"I think for Rose's sake we should travel together."

He shook his head. "Lady, I know you want my baby, but you'll never get her from me."

"I don't want to steal Rose."

"You want something. I can feel it."

She slowly nodded. "Yes. I do. I want you to travel with me to the next place, and be my cover."

"I don't even know how I got here. I don't want to travel again, whatever that means." Maybe she'd done it. Maybe it was her—the woman—who had pulled him forward through time, and not the baby. He desperately hoped it wasn't Auburn who had somehow worked a magic spell to draw him to her. He could be stuck with her!

"We'll just head west," she said soothingly.

He'd heard that one before. Everyone always wanted to go west, for gold, for open land, for a new start.

"What are you running from?"

"An ex-fiancé. A wealthy ex-fiancé, whom I discovered has a shady past. I'm a little afraid that he'll find me." She took a breath. "And I'm not ready for that."

He held Rose's carrier tightly in one hand, her sack of belongings in the other. Had Auburn brought him here because she wanted protection from a man? Needed a husband? All he knew was that he didn't trust this woman and her big eyes at all. "Because?"

"He'll be embarrassed that I stood him up. And it's worse because my family owes their livelihood to him. I've always enjoyed a privileged lifestyle, but I thought my parents earned their wealth on their own. The week before the wedding, I learned that they had done deals over time with my fiancé. I began to feel uncomfortably like the fatted calf. Which sounds horrible because my family loves me. But I wanted to make it on my own in the world, not belong to someone. Does that sound crazy?"

He didn't know. Women made agreements to marry for a dozen reasons, most of them complicated, some ridiculous, but they seemed to make sense to the female mind. It was a complex issue. Polly had married him, she always said, because she couldn't love a man who couldn't manage her high spirits and her energy. But he hadn't managed Polly; she'd managed him. He'd enjoyed the light of her spirit, letting it flow over him. She could have married a lot better than a gunslinger, even though he'd changed everything about himself to win Polly. Her family had never forgiven him his past, though they loved her dearly. Shame had been written all over their faces anytime they saw him. They couldn't believe he had won their daughter's heart.

He couldn't believe he had, either.

But right now, this woman was standing in his way. She claimed to need him, and truthfully, he could use her, too, but only if she wasn't planning to make off with his baby. She struck him as the type who didn't make easy attachments, though he wasn't sure why he felt that way. It was just a feeling he had, and he always went with his hunches. "Listen, I like traveling alone."

She perked up. "So do I! It's really more economical, isn't it? You don't have to share anything, you can go where you want to…." Her face fell. "On the other hand, it can be lonely."

"I'm never lonely," he fibbed. He'd been lonely on the ranch after Polly died, desperately so.

"Well, you're brave." She shrugged. "You and Rose can take the backseat, if you must feel alone. I'll be in the front, and we can ignore each other."

He didn't think he could totally ignore her, any more than he could ignore a wasp stinging his buttocks. "How far west are you going?"

"I was thinking New Mexico," she said, her tone breezy. "But you can choose, if you like."

"I don't really care," he said with a growl, stopping himself from saying, *but if you try to take my baby, I'll find you.* "One condition," he said.

"What?"

He took a long, hard look at her, trying to see inside her soul. He had pretty good success with reading people; if you didn't have that sixth sense, you could wind up dead. "No more mothering this baby."

She drew herself up, clearly hurt. "Fine, cowboy. You can take care of that child all by your little old self."

"Good."

"Fine." She swept past him on the stairwell. "Let me grab my things. I don't have much, and I'm paid up through the month here."

Now was his moment to take off, get away from her and her spell. But she piqued his curiosity in the worst way. What if she was somehow instrumental to his existence in this century? He had to find the key to getting himself sent back. "How do you pay by the month at a place like this?"

"By understanding the travel industry. Anyway, you let me handle the arrangements, cowboy. You mind the angel."

Fine. He didn't really want to know any more about her than he had to, anyway.

Only her traveling secret, and she'd just now given herself away. Auburn understood the travel industry, both in this dimension and some others.

He felt pretty smart at figuring her out so easily.

MEN COULD BE IDIOTS. Auburn tried not to swear under her breath as she tossed her Louis Vuitton luggage into the trunk of her car, annoyed that Dillinger had tried to leave her high and dry. Steal his baby? Hah! She wasn't completely certain that was Dillinger's child, but he'd turned bearlike, protective of his cub.

She wouldn't touch his silly old baby, if he was going to be such an ass about it. "Get in the back," she told him crossly, "and strap that carrier in correctly, please."

She sounded bossy and she knew it, but he complied, fumbling a bit with the straps before correctly tightening the baby backward in the seat. Auburn smiled a little at Rose, stiffening when she caught Dillinger looking at her. "You're getting better at that," she said airily.

"Like you're an expert at it, yourself."

Turning on the car engine, she said, "I was trying to give you a compliment. Obviously, you're the kind of man whose ego won't let you accept one gracefully."

"Probably." The rearview mirror showed him gazing with interest at the buildings downtown as they passed, not paying a whole lot of attention to her as she drove from the city. Auburn picked the highway marked West and pressed the pedal as hard as the speed limit would allow.

THIS WAS LIKE A magic carpet ride, or a train that could go full-speed across the country. Dillinger was fascinated by the way Auburn flew past the cars and signs on the highway. It was amazing! There were things overhead she called airplanes—he didn't let on that he had barely heard of flying machines—and so much to see that his head was whirling. She *was* the reason he was here, he was positive.

He had to convince her to send him and Rose back. They were not suited for living like this. First, he had to return Rose to her rightful mother, even if it meant helping them financially. He felt certain no mother would abandon a baby on his porch unless the woman was destitute.

The only thing he couldn't understand was why the mother had chosen *his* porch. He was miles from town. He had a bad reputation. He didn't darken the doorway of a church. And this was no frontier baby. Her clothes were store-bought. Her socks were knit of the finest lace and cotton, not rough country socks made for warmth and work, like his. Rose should be placed with a family of wealth, not stay with him, if he couldn't manage to find her birth mother. He knew it was imperative that he get the baby home as fast as possible.

What if he could talk Auburn into taking him and Rose back home to the ranch, and going with them? She said she needed to hide away. She'd be safe at his ranch. No one would ever find her there.

But did he want the opinionated woman in his home, where Polly had brought him such warmth and contentment?

For Rose's sake, he could do it.

He'd opened his mouth to broach the question, when suddenly he felt himself being jerked against the seat belt.

PIERRE TOSSED THE EARRING across the room. He'd fallen asleep in a chair in Dillinger's den, and had awakened annoyed that the man hadn't yet returned. The snow outside was piling up, making a mess of the dirt road. If he wasn't careful, he'd get snowed in and trapped here for God only knew how long. Anger built inside him. He felt outsmarted by the gunslinger, and he hated it. Maybe the man had planned to be gone for weeks, months.

Pierre felt bad for throwing his sister's earring. He picked up the delicate bauble again, giving it one last shake. His heart heavy, he vowed to return next week, when Dillinger might be home and the snow and ice not threatening to encase the house in a chilly tomb. Why the man chose to live out here when he could have lived in town was puzzling, but he'd had Polly all to himself this way. A beautiful flower like his sister hadn't deserved to wilt out here in the uncivilized wilderness.

Pierre put the earring back on the writing desk, staring at it for a long time, tempted to take the trinket with him. Maybe the charcoal drawing of his sister would ease the ache in his heart more. But no, it didn't truly capture the fire Polly had possessed.

He left everything just as it had been, so the gunslinger would never suspect someone had been waiting here, planning to kill him.

Chapter Four

Dillinger tried not to gasp as his body strained against the seat belt. It was as if he were being jerked by a strong, invisible hand trying to tear him from the car. Only the straps kept him restrained.

"Is something wrong?" Auburn asked, staring at him in the rearview mirror.

"No," he said, grinding out the word.

She checked the road, then glanced back to his reflection. "Are you sure? You don't look good."

He unhooked the belt, relieved when the pressure subsided.

"You have to wear that," Auburn said. "It's against the law not to wear a seat belt."

He grimaced at the pain in his stomach and across his chest. "Do you think that's a strange thing to tell a gunslinger?" He checked the belt again. This time it was acting as it should. Maybe the thing had malfunctioned.

Maybe there hadn't been anything supernatural trying to drag him from this car.

"You know, about that gunslinger business, maybe we should figure out some other livelihood for you, when people ask what you do," Auburn said, her voice bright.

"Why? Who's going to care?"

She shook her head. "No one, most likely. But if anyone asks, why don't you tell them you work for... I don't know." Her gaze lit on him in the mirror again. "You can say you're an unemployed model."

He laughed. "I don't think so."

"Well, just say you're a ranch owner."

"I am."

"You are?"

She sounded so shocked that he frowned. "I told you. I own a ranch outside of Christmas River."

"But I looked that up. There's no such town."

"Care to place a wager on that?"

"No."

She could be quite the shrew. He tried to relax in the magic vehicle, which had a material top that she said pulled back to let in sunshine and fresh air and the feeling of freedom.

"You felt it, didn't you?"

She'd caught him off guard. "Felt what?"

Auburn moved one finger in the air in a slow circle.

"If you hadn't been wearing that seat belt, you would have gone airborne again."

Polly wouldn't have hounded him so. This woman had no qualms about doing it. "The contraption simply malfunctioned."

"You felt it, and now you know I was telling you the truth."

He didn't care. He was so sleepy all he could do was send a fast glance at Rose to make certain she was still happy and nestled in her carrier. Fear suddenly hit his gut. "Do me a favor," he said, fighting to keep his eyelids open. "If something happens to me, take care of Rose."

"Nothing's going to happen to you," Auburn said, trying to sound soothing. "You just have a bad habit of levitating."

"Promise," he insisted.

"I'm not really cut out for taking care of a baby. I've got problems of my own."

He couldn't argue with her any longer. Unconsciousness pulled at him, forbidding him to stay awake, as much as he would have enjoyed telling her that he'd never seen a woman so cut out to be a mother.

Except maybe Polly.

And that worried him, too. He fell asleep, his soul tortured by thoughts of what might have been and what should have been.

WHAT WOULD IT HURT to swing by this place he called Christmas River? Maybe the answers to his problem were there. Auburn punched "Christmas" into her GPS system. They weren't far from a town called Christy River—maybe he was confused from all the whirling around he engaged in. It was just a fast detour from where they planned to go, but they certainly had no schedule and nowhere definitive to be. Going to such a remote place might even help her put some distance between her and her fiancé. The cowboy wouldn't awaken, not for a while, so she couldn't ask him, but she had a feeling he'd be happy to get home.

She knew something was wrong with him, knew he knew it, too. He didn't want to admit his fear, but for a man who claimed to routinely face down killers, what was bugging him now appeared to be bigger than anything he'd dealt with before.

He'd asked her about taking care of Rose, and for the first time, concern swept through Auburn. She couldn't take on a baby if something happened to the hunky cowboy. Her eyes went to him in the mirror. He slept with his head tipped back against the seat, an ungraceful position, which had no bearing whatsoever on his sex appeal. She liked her men tall, dark and handsome, with a dash of mystery thrown in, so Dillinger was everything she would never have been able to resist in a man.

And yet she would have forced herself to, which was

why she'd chosen the supersafe Bradley Jackson for her fiancé, a dreadful mistake that hadn't been safe at all. Her parents owned the popular McGinnis Perfumes. She'd proudly worked as a vice president at the company. Bradley had been the CFO.

But three weeks before the wedding matters had gone terribly wrong, and she'd learned things about the company—and specifically her own family—that she'd never known.

It still hurt to think about it. Her parents said Bradley basically owned the company now. They'd hit a snag during hard times and Bradley had financed their debt through his own company. The wonderful perfumes Auburn remembered her grandmother carefully fashioning to enrich a woman's life were phased out, replaced with cheaply made imitations. Every bottle sold generated huge profit. In this way, Bradley was receiving revenue from the loan, which her parents had never had to pay back.

The debt would have all been swept clean with her marriage to Bradley. She still smarted under the realization that the man she'd loved—and believed loved her—had actually owned her and her family lock, stock and barrel. No woman wanted to feel like that.

"You're deep in thought," Dillinger said, startling her.

"You're awake."

He grunted.

"Do you feel better?"

"I didn't feel bad." He glanced down at the baby. "She sure does sleep peacefully when she sleeps."

The infant probably derived comfort from Dillinger's deep voice. Auburn turned her gaze back to the road, vowing not to allow the rearview mirror to continue to lure her to stare at the hunk in her backseat.

"What does it feel like?" Auburn asked.

"I'd like to pretend I don't know what you're talking about, but since I'm completely at a loss as to what's happening to me, I guess I'll just say it feels strange."

"Like you're having a hypoglycemic attack?"

"What's that?"

"Low blood sugar."

"I don't know what that is. Sorry, my medical knowledge ends around 1892."

She couldn't help it; she stared at him in the mirror. "Part of me believes that you really think you're from another place and time."

He just shook his head, and she went back to driving. "Listen, maybe you should see a doctor," she suggested worriedly.

"You mean you think I'm dangerous. That my mind is addled."

She refused to meet his gaze; she could feel him looking at her in the mirror. "I don't know what to think."

He sighed. "Where are we going?"

"To Christy River."

"I'm from Christmas River."

"Can't it be the same thing? Maybe the Google map has a misprint. It does that sometimes."

"Google map?"

"Never mind." She pulled into a Sonic drive-through, ordered a couple of burgers, and by the time they were finished—the cowboy wolfed his—Rose was awake and ready for her bottle. Together they managed the whole burp, diaper, comfort routine. Chilly as it was outside, Rose didn't mind being put back into her snug carrier for another nap.

"She's tired from traveling," Dillinger observed.

"Oh, traveling does that to everyone." Auburn got into the driver's seat and started the car.

"I meant, traveling through time."

She frowned. "Listen, let's play a little game, okay?"

"I don't really like games."

"Who was the most famous person of 1892?"

"I don't know." He shrugged. "Lord Tennyson died in October. I like his poems. Some of them had to do with the Knights of the Round Table. My wife enjoyed reading to me."

"Can you read?"

"Of course I can read!" He scowled at her. "It's a pleasure to have one's wife read aloud at fireside!"

"Sorry, sorry." Jeez, he could be sensitive about certain things. Auburn didn't know if Tennyson had died in 1892 or not, but Dillinger sounded pretty knowledgeable so she let it pass. "Who was the president?"

"Grover Cleveland was just reelected. Third term, though not consecutively. He came back to beat President Benjamin Harrison. Other than that, I didn't pay too much attention. We tend to set our own rules out West. Not sure what he knows about ranching, so I let him run the country and I run my ranch."

He could have studied 1892 and become well versed in the history. But why did he keep levitating?

What if he really was from another time? Auburn pulled out of the Sonic parking lot. She'd be a fool if she started believing this man's wild story, she told herself. She'd just discovered how painful it was when someone you trusted lied to you, and she had her guard up. Planned on keeping it up.

"So what really happened to your wife?"

Dillinger's heart clenched with familiar pain at the topic. He didn't want to talk about it. Still, he sensed genuine curiosity not borne from meanness in Auburn's question. "She died of pneumonia. I couldn't get the doctor out to our ranch fast enough. Don't know what he could have done, anyway. All those tinctures they give seem pretty useless to me. It started out as a cold, though I kept the house warm as toast. I never left her side." He shuddered, remembering the fever that had swept through Polly. He'd kept her wrapped, made sure not a draft entered the house. Tried to feed her soup he made himself.

Nothing had helped.

"I'm so sorry," Auburn said. "I can tell you miss her."

"I don't miss her so much that I'm unhinged, if that's what you're thinking."

"I didn't think that at all!"

"Sure you did," Dillinger said.

Auburn's eyes met his in the mirror, but he looked away before he could see the pity there. "She was an angel," he said, "and now she's with the angels. I really couldn't have kept her long. I realize that now."

"But now you have Rose," Auburn said.

"But for how long?" Dillinger asked, gently touching the soft, fine hairs on the baby's head. He was getting awfully attached to a child that wasn't his. He didn't even know why her mother had left her with him. No doubt the people of Christmas River would say he'd stolen her, the same way they'd accused him of murdering Polly.

"I hope she'll stay with me," he said quietly. "She's all I've got right now."

"Where would she go?" Auburn asked. "It's not like she can walk away."

Dillinger shook his head. Auburn couldn't possibly understand the demons that drove him, and why this little angel was his only connection to the world he knew.

Chapter Five

They got out of the car in Christy River just a few hours later. Dillinger shook his head. "This isn't it."

Auburn was disappointed. "Are you sure?"

"Yes." Even if everything wasn't much more modern, changed over and new, he would recognize his hometown. "The topography isn't even the same."

She held Rose tucked to her chest, surveying the road where they'd stopped. He liked watching her care for the baby, but he couldn't get over the astonishing sight of hundreds of cars flying along the highway. "We rode horses over land like this," he murmured.

She smiled at him. "You're an old-fashioned guy."

"I think I'm fairly progressive."

"What made you become a gunslinger?" she asked softly, and he forced himself to consider the question and give her an honest answer, even if he really didn't want to talk about a way of life he'd given up for Polly.

"I met one man who didn't believe in peaceful solutions," he said. "After that, it seemed I was offered plenty of jobs the law couldn't handle—or didn't want to handle—on their own. And the pay was good." He shrugged. "Let's get one of those burger things, on my nickel. Being a new father is making me hungry. I want to eat like Rose does, every three hours."

"We can grab something at that McDonald's," Auburn suggested, getting in the car. "It's pretty nonnutritious food, but I do love their French fries."

He got in the car, made sure Rose was secure in her seat.

"Would you ever tell me about how you did your job?" Auburn asked as their eyes met over Rose's carrier.

"No," he said quietly. "Some stories aren't good in the retelling."

She didn't believe he was from 1892. How could she understand anything about his life? Dillinger let Rose grab his finger, smiling when she held on to it with determination. "She's a tough little girl," he said. "A survivor."

Auburn started the car and pulled into traffic. He was surprised by how comfortable he was, letting her drive him around. Where he was from, the man usually handled the team of horses, drove the buckboard. He couldn't remember Polly driving anything, although she'd been an excellent horsewoman. Polly had been more delicate than Auburn. It was strange how Auburn had changed since she'd left her employment at the theater; she was softer, more feminine. He wondered about her family, why they didn't seem concerned about her being off on her own.

A sudden shrill ringing startled him and Rose.

"Sorry," Auburn said, "I have to take this. It's my sister, Cherie."

He watched, astonished, as she pulled a small black box from her purse and began talking into it. She listened, laughed, then talked some more. It was amazing. Everything one wanted to say could be done instantly, not in a letter or handwritten message.

She put the object away. "She's telling everyone I've gone to Florida to think things over."

"Can I look at that thing?"

"This? It's an iPhone," she said, handing it to him. "Don't you have a cell phone?"

"No." He stared at it, amazed by all the strange markings. "And you can talk to someone on this."

"Anywhere in the world."

He blinked. "Anywhere?"

"Yes."

He handed it back to her. "How do you know how to reach someone?"

"Usually you know their number and have it in your phone list. If not, you can look it up in a phone book or on the Internet. There are maps of everything, anything you want to know at all, right here."

He considered that. "So, if there was such a thing as Christmas River, that phone would show it."

"Right. And there's nothing listed. I checked."

So the town name had changed. He was going to have to find out what the new name was, or be forever lost. "I have to know what happened to my town," he told her.

Auburn's gaze met his in the mirror. "Yeah. About that. I don't know how we will. Google didn't pick up anything when I looked it up. There's a San Christmas River in California."

"Texas," he stated, and she sighed.

"I'm sorry. It's not referenced."

There was no way a town suddenly never existed. "That doesn't make sense."

She pulled into the restaurant parking lot. "What do you want?"

"Nothing," he said slowly, and she turned around to look at him.

"You said you were famished, cowboy!"

"I was." Now he felt somewhat empty. Tired. This Christy River wasn't his home. He might never get back there. If it didn't exist now, no one would believe it had existed then.

He glared at Auburn, noticing her sympathetic expression. "Get some of those French fries you love and quit staring at me with that 'clearly he's crazy' look."

"Confused. Not crazy." She ordered two Cokes, two fries and a few burgers. "You said you traveled a lot—"

"Before I married Polly. After that, we stayed on the ranch together. I didn't travel so much that I forgot where I lived."

"Okay, okay." She handed him back food he didn't want, yet the grumbling of his stomach made him grab one of the French fry things she bragged about. "This is weird food."

"Yeah, well. Road treats." Auburn pulled away from the drive-through window. He couldn't believe someone would actually hand food through a window for a person to eat. When he was away from home, he ate at diners or homes where people served food for money. No one ever shoved it at him in a bag through a window.

"We could have used something like this on cattle drives."

"I don't know where to go now," Auburn murmured. "I was so sure I was onto something."

He drank the fizzy liquid, wrinkling his nose. "That's terrible!"

"Really? You don't like cola?"

He shuddered. "I prefer water from the spring on my ranch."

She turned to stare at him. "If you had a spring, do you recall the name of it?"

"It was just a spring on my property."

"Do you recall the county you lived in? What city was next to Christmas River?"

"We lived in Montwest County. The closest town was Chapel, but that was a good day's journey by horseback. Of course there were no trains out there, not these things that you have now." He'd been fascinated by the DART transportation as they'd left Dallas.

"So you lived west of Chapel?"

"East." He ate the burger. It wasn't as good as what he'd get in a chop house or even on a trail drive, but it passed as food.

"We could head that way if you like."

After a moment, he shook his head. "No. Go on to where you need to go."

"I really have no place to be. I'm just…seeing the country."

"How long will you run from your problems?" he asked, curious. Everybody avoided things, some longer than others. But a bad engagement seemed like something easily fixed.

On the other hand, he was definitely on the outs with Polly's family. He guessed there were some situations that couldn't be fixed peacefully.

"I'd like to give it two more weeks." Auburn turned south on the highway. "Then I'll go home and tell everyone I can't be the answer to their problems."

"Do you have brothers, or just a sister?"

"No other siblings. It's just me and Cherie."

He caught the wistful tone in her voice. "You wanted a bigger family?"

"Don't you have family?"

It had been only him. His parents had died young. He'd been raised on cattle drives by sympathetic ranchers who took an interest in him. He'd learned how to shoot, how to hunt, how to be a man. "No," he said, "not everyone wants one."

That was the untruth of the century. He'd wanted one with Polly desperately, but he wasn't about to confide that to Auburn. She'd look at him with those sympathetic eyes, and he didn't want that.

"I don't think I'll ever marry," Auburn said, sounding very cheerful about it. "Men are quite needy."

"You're just put out right now because your man wasn't what you wanted. All women want a family."

Her gaze settled on him. "That's a sexist remark."

"A what?"

"A… Something you say when you don't think much of the other person, most particularly a person of the opposite sex."

"I think a lot of you." He frowned. It was true. She was strong, independent. Caring. He admired those things in a woman. "You seem like a nice lady. Just a bit down on your luck."

"Anyway," she said, "in this day and age, one doesn't say things like *all women want marriage,* or *a woman should only stay home and take care of children.*"

He was shocked. "What else would she want to do? Other than the queen of England, who is an exception. Queen Victoria must rule her country, of course."

Auburn considered his argument. She had to know he was correct, but he sensed her marshaling a new line of debate. He wasn't disappointed when she asked, "Well, how would you feel if I said all men are cheats?"

"It has nothing to do with me, so I wouldn't take offense." He shrugged. "Still, I guess you don't like me to say you want a family. Even though you do, I won't say it anymore."

She rolled her eyes. "It's best not to sound pigheaded when you talk to ladies. You can get a purse upside your head for that. I mean, *I* understand you, at least a little, but someone else you meet might not take remarks like that in stride."

Polly had never called him pigheaded. He was surprised Auburn would. Dillinger didn't know what to think about that, so he pulled his hat low on his forehead—the universal signal for *leave me alone,* and hoped Shakespeare's girl would take the hint and cease her tirade on how a man should treat a woman.

He wasn't certain he liked this new breed of lady.

And yet he wasn't totally sure he didn't.

TWO HOURS LATER, when she was certain that Dillinger was hiding under his hat and not sleeping, and when she could tell that little Rose was about send up the feeding alarm, Auburn pulled over for gas. "We should make a plan for the night, Dillinger."

Panic seemed to flare in his eyes as he released Rose from her carrier and cradled her to his chest. "What do you suggest?"

"Well, there are hotels along the highway, any number of them. We could do a bed-and-breakfast, but we don't have a reservation and those might be full, since it's the Christmas season."

"It's up to you."

She eyed the horizon. "How about that Hilton?"

"It's better than the ground."

He made a bottle—he was getting good at that— and began to feed Rose. Auburn smiled. "You two are becoming a great team. She hardly even cries now." The baby had no reason to; if she let out so much as a squeak, Dillinger was right there to attend to her needs. He'd gotten the crying thing down quickly, hadn't had to be told twice. Rose's security level had gone up greatly, knowing that her needs would be addressed rapidly.

"I'm a peaceful man, remember? Crying babies are not peaceful."

Auburn got back inside the car. "I'll get us two rooms, close together, and we can—"

"One," he said. "One room."

She turned to look at him. "Why one?"

"So I can keep an eye on you."

She raised her brows. "I don't need an eye kept on me."

"What if your fiancé shows up?"

"He won't. Not yet." Auburn shrugged. "And if he does, it'll be messy, but nothing I can't handle."

"Still." Dillinger gave her a meaningful look. "Surely they have a big room with bunks or something."

"I'm not sleeping in a bunk!" She pulled out from the gas station and headed to the Hilton. It wasn't far up the road, so by the time she parked the car, Rose was done and in the process of letting out a good, reverberating burp, which made Dillinger laugh, and that made Auburn smile. She loved hearing him laugh. Most of the time he was so stodgy and deep, but the baby could always coax some lightness out of him. "You stay here. I'll go check if there's a vacancy."

"I'll go with you." Dillinger got out of the car, the baby firmly tucked against his chest.

Auburn put her hands on her hips. "What is your deal?"

"What do you mean?" He tried to look innocent, but twenty-four hours with Dillinger had taught Auburn that innocent wasn't his easiest expression.

"You act like I'm going to disappear on you!"

He winced. "Look, I hardly think that's likely, since I'm sitting in your car. I'm just interested in how everything works in your world." His square chin jutted out just a bit with resolute firmness. "Is that all right with you?"

"Something tells me this isn't about curiosity, but whatever…" Auburn walked inside the hotel and headed to the desk. A young girl, maybe twenty-one, stood ready to assist patrons.

"I'd like a room, please," Auburn said, "if you have one."

"Certainly. The size you were looking for?" The girl's eyes wandered over Dillinger and the baby.

"The biggest you have, please," Dillinger said politely. Auburn glared at him.

"I can handle this!" she said.

"I know! I'm just trying to be a gentleman."

The hotel clerk blinked. "If I could get your name—"

"Mr. and Mrs. Robert Smith," Dillinger said, pulling his wallet from his duster. "Does it have a bathtub or is a bath extra?"

The girl's eyes went wide. "Yes, sir, there is a bathtub. It comes standard with the room."

Auburn looked at him. "Robert?"

"Yes, dear?" He returned her stare.

"Why do we need a bathtub?" Auburn asked sweetly.

"Because the baby needs a bath," he pointed out just as sweetly, "and I wouldn't mind one myself."

Auburn couldn't argue with that logic. Not that he looked particularly like he needed a bath, but she would have banked on him being a shower kind of guy. She wondered if they had showers in 1892—and then caught herself. She was beginning to believe his poppycock! How dumb could she be? This would be even worse than believing Bradley when he'd told her that he was a financier. And that he loved her, when all the while he was ensnaring her family corporation for his own greedy purposes.

"Maybe I should get a second room so you and the baby can sleep soundly, Robert," she said.

He put money on the desk, shaking his head. "We sleep like rocks, I promise. You won't bother us a bit." His smile took the counter girl into his confidence. "My wife snores terribly."

Auburn's jaw dropped. But then her gaze fell on the money he'd left on the counter.

It was all newly minted, crisp paper. Not money from 1892. Why hadn't she realized that before, when he'd paid for Rose's diapers and things at the Wal-Mart? Auburn marched outside, not even bothering to hear which room would be theirs.

Dillinger joined her a second later. "Would you mind telling me what you were doing back there?" she demanded.

"Keeping an eye on you, in case you decided to pack up and leave us in the night."

"Oh, I see." The thought hadn't occurred to her before, but maybe it should have. "Look, I agreed to help you with the baby—"

"And I agreed to protect you—"

She'd forgotten she'd mentioned that to him. It was kind of nice that he'd taken her seriously. All she'd really wanted was to make certain little Rose was in good hands. Now she knew that no matter whose baby she really was, Dillinger was always going to do the best he could by her. Which was kind of sexy, Auburn had to admit, though she didn't allow herself to linger on that thought.

They reached her car. "Cowboy, you and I should part ways in the morning. I can drop you off wherever you want to be."

He looked hurt. "Have I offended you in some way?"

He had, but she didn't really want to go into the details. "I'm just used to taking care of myself."

"Did I interfere with that?"

"Paying for the room back there. Giving us a fake name." Auburn shook her head. "You worry me. You're awfully good at telling fibs."

He laughed. "I'm used to giving aliases. If people knew I was in their town, they'd wonder who I was after. Whoever I was hunting would get a jump on me. What kind of gunslinger would I have been if I didn't know how to sneak up on my target?"

She didn't know. She didn't care. Couldn't care, anyway, because she was starting to slip under his spell and believe the outrageous stories he spun for her. "Dillinger, if you're from 1892, why is your money the same as mine?"

He looked perplexed as he pulled Rose's sack of belongings from the car. "My money *should* be the same as yours. It's marked with Treasury Secretary William Windom's signature, though soon enough I suspect the new guy will get his name put on it."

She shook her head. "Can I see some of your money?"

"Sure." He pulled out a wad of cash, handed it to her.

"There has to be a thousand dollars here," she said, startled. "All new."

"It's not that new," he stated. "Like I said, the new treasury secretary will have his name put on it just as soon as Mr. Cleveland chooses him."

"No, see, it doesn't say 1892, or any time of any other century. All the bills are clearly freshly minted from the twenty-first century."

He shook his head. "No, every bill I've got clearly says William Windom, who is the current treasury secretary. I've been saving my money for about a year, hoping that Polly and I…"

His voice drifted off. He seemed so sad that Auburn wished she hadn't argued over the money. Yet it was important. "Why do you have so much money on you? No one usually keeps that much. It was much safer and efficient to use plastic."

"Don't trust banks much. You wouldn't, either, after Reconstruction. Kept my money in gold and other such things. Then I was planning to buy some more land. We were also wanting to have a child. This isn't all I have, but it's all that was in my pocket when I—" His face turned strange, almost an ashen color as he reached to put the money roll back under his duster. Auburn watched, stunned, as he pulled a golden earring from his pocket.

"How the hell—" He broke off, staring at it.

"What? What?" she asked. He didn't seem at all happy to see the jewelry. Quickly, he felt inside his pocket, even handing her Rose so he could check everywhere on his person. "What is it?"

"It's Polly's earring," he murmured. "I'm sure I put them back on the desk. But I must have had one in my hand when I went to answer the door."

"Who was at the door?" Auburn asked softly, holding the baby close. The look in Dillinger's eyes was scaring her. He seemed sad, maybe even anguished.

"I told you. It was Rose," he said. "She was on the porch in a basket. If I hadn't gone to the door, she would have died. The snow was coming down fast. I was worried about my cattle." He stared at the earring, clearly remembering something painful.

"May I see it?" she asked.

"No!" he snapped, so harshly that she jumped.

He sighed, recognizing his rudeness. "I'm sorry. It's just a bauble. Of course you may see it." He gave it to her, his gaze on her face as she inspected it.

"It's lovely, Dillinger. It's your wife's, isn't it?"

"It was." He took back the baby. "Let's go to the room. If you still want to leave me behind in the morning, I completely understand. We've taken up enough of your time with looking for a town that obviously doesn't exist anymore."

As his fingers brushed hers, he reached to take the earring. And suddenly Auburn saw it. She saw the ranch and the animals and his wife sitting by the fire smiling at him, ready to read him a book. She saw the plates on the table and the old-fashioned candles illuminating the room. Though it was cold outside, it was cozy and warm where they sat. Dillinger had an expression of happiness she'd never seen on his face, completely unlike the worried frown that had creased his brow since she'd met him.

"I see it," she gasped. "I saw your house! And Polly!"

He gave her an odd look. "How can you?"

"I don't know! It was brief, and it's gone now. But I saw it!"

He shook his head. "I don't believe in visions. On the other hand, if you're the instrument to my being here, please send Rose and me back."

"It wasn't a vision! Well, maybe it was," Auburn

said. "I never had one before so I wouldn't know. But your wife was beautiful. She wore a long green dress. You had white plates on the table. There was a round rag rug in front of a stone fireplace, and two candlesticks on the table. She held a book—"

"Stop!" He glared at her. "Don't say another word."

Chapter Six

There was so much Auburn couldn't explain about the cowboy, but she knew with total acceptance of what she'd seen that Dillinger was telling the truth. He was from another place and time. He didn't know how he'd gotten here. There was no other way to explain his sudden levitation—he still didn't want to admit it had happened—or the fact that she and everyone else saw his money as completely normal for this time, when he saw it as paper from his own time. His dress, his manners—he wasn't faking any of it. His knowledge of the time period was something he was completely comfortable with.

"It's the baby," Auburn said breathlessly. "She brought you here."

"Witch," Dillinger murmured. "I'm beginning to think you are a witch. How can you blame a small and helpless baby? She can't even feed herself, much less do what you're suggesting."

They walked inside their hotel room, keeping distance between them. A roll-away bed had been placed in the unit, which was large and spacious. The baby could sleep surrounded by pillows for safety if she protested being in her carrier. Dillinger locked the door behind them, and Auburn turned to look at him.

"I saw you," she said. "I know you're telling the truth."

"How?" he asked, taking off his duster.

"Because you were happy," she said softly.

He laughed. Took off his blue work shirt to reveal a broad, masculine chest. "I *was* happy," he said, "and now I don't want to talk about this anymore. I'm going to take a bath."

"A shower," Auburn murmured. "You'll probably want a shower." She should have offered him one at her penthouse, but hadn't trusted him enough to do so. Had been too stunned when he'd flown into the air. What was that all about?

"I'll figure it out."

He left her alone in the room with the baby, his back so broad and muscled that she instantly longed to place her cheek against it, wrap her arms around his waist—

Am I nuts? He didn't trust her in the least. Telling him that she'd seen him and his wife in his home had only put a big red flag in his mind that she wasn't honest. He thought she was toying with him.

She picked Rose up for comfort, staring into her face.

"Is it you?" she asked. "Did you bring your cowboy here to keep him safe?"

Was he here to stay?

Suddenly, Auburn hoped so.

DILLINGER FIGURED OUT the shower knobs easily, turned on the hot water and stood under it, letting the tears flow down his cheeks. Auburn had described Polly and their home perfectly—and it had hurt. The memories were painful, like a burn from a branding iron.

He pulled his head from under the water, turned to let it run over his back. If he'd been dragged to this time, could Polly be nearby? It was a tantalizing fantasy, even as he knew it wasn't possible. He was still alive; Rose was living. Polly had died. She was nowhere but in heaven. Yet he wanted so much to think that somehow she had brought him forward in time to be with her.

What about Auburn? How could she have seen everything so clearly, even to the color of Polly's favorite dress? Lucky guess?

No. Unless he'd talked in his sleep, or she'd tricked it out of him somehow, Auburn had perfectly described his and Polly's favorite place to sit at the end of the day. Together.

A knock on the door made him jump. "What?"

"You're not the only one who needs to use the lavatory!"

He sighed. A gentleman would have allowed the lady to go first. She could hardly take the baby down to the lobby and perform her necessary functions. And he knew Auburn would never leave Rose. In his haste to withdraw from her, he'd forgotten all about her needs.

Very unlike him to be that much of an ass. She would very likely give him what-for about it.

Toweling off quickly, he threw open the door. "Sorry," he said, "I wasn't—what?"

Auburn stared at the glory of the man naked. She'd never seen a male quite like this. Oh, he had a towel around his waist, but that hid very little. Amazing muscles and sinew and a trim, hard waist, shoulders that were strong from labor… Her mouth dried out, her knees buckled slightly.

"I need to wash my clothes," he said, his tone apologetic. "I don't mean to offend you."

She blinked, hardly offended.

"I do beg your pardon," he said, "but if you would just turn around, I could grab a blanket off the bed and wrap up—"

She flew into the bathroom and slammed the door, unable to speak. *Holy cow, I've got the hots for a ghost! How creepy is that?*

She'd never seen any man who looked like Dillinger did, all dark and bad boy and yet curiously genteel. Sexy and forbidding and somehow sensitive…

She was going to lose her mind sleeping in the same room with him.

"Maybe he doesn't look so great in the morning," she muttered, feeling hopeless because if anyone had a rough morning appearance, it was going to be her and not him.

She could sleep with her makeup on.

"Forget that," she said, turning on the shower. "He doesn't trust me, anyway. Makeup won't help."

"Are you okay in there?"

She stiffened. "Yes! Why?"

"Because I hear you talking to someone."

She blushed. "Um, no. Must have been in the next room."

"You're not stirring up any spells in there, are you?"

She wrapped a towel tightly around herself—forget the modesty—and jerked open the door. "Look, cowboy. You have to get one thing straight—I don't do spells. I don't do anything at all. I found you when you suddenly appeared in the middle of our stage show, and rescued you from bumbling around in the twenty-first century. I'm not the one who flails around in the air, either. Okay? No more of that witch talk."

He was staring at her legs below the white towel. Well, surely he'd seen a female leg before! She began to wonder if he was counting her freckles, of which she had plenty. "Is there something wrong?"

"I— No."

He averted his gaze. She watched as his eyes seemed to slowly move of their own accord to her shoulders, taking a slow journey from one to the other. What if he were to run his hands along her shoulders in the same manner, slow and mesmerized? She grew soft and dreamy just imagining his touch on her skin.

"If you're finished staring at me, can we get back to the problem at hand?" she demanded.

"Problem?" He swallowed, his Adam's apple bobbing.

"I don't like you calling me a witch or a sorceress, or thinking I had anything to do with your being here. Got that?" She raised her chin, meeting his gaze.

"How could you possibly describe my home and my wife if you aren't—"

"Believe me, I'm not happy about it," she snapped. "Let's get over it and move on. You don't call me a witch and I don't call you a…a thief."

"Thief!"

"Of that baby."

Rose began wailing and the argument died instantly. Dillinger hurried to her, talking softly and sweetly, completely unlike how he spoke to Auburn. She wrinkled her nose, her feelings a bit hurt, decided the fact that they were both wearing nothing but towels wasn't a sign of good things to come, since they barely got along. She went to take a long shower.

WHEN SHE FINISHED blow-drying her hair, Auburn stepped into the room to find the cowboy and the baby gone. Her keys were still there, as was her purse, so she knew he hadn't swiped her car. Not that he would swipe a rose-colored convertible, but with them having harsh words for each other, her first thought was that he'd decided to follow through on his promise to get out of her hair.

He might have decided to take another room, though. Worry jumped inside her. She didn't want him to do that.

"And why don't I?" she asked herself. "Am I just a wee bit too interested?"

It was dumb. Grabbing some clothes from her suitcase, she dressed quickly. If she was starting to get a soft heart for the man, she was heading for trouble.

The door unlocked, then opened. She jumped to her feet, glad she'd pulled on her clothes. "Where did you go?" she asked, hating that she sounded interested. *As if I can't bear for him to leave my sight even for a second.*

"Rose and I took a little stroll. She told me she needed some fresh air, and I told her I needed to clear my head."

He'd put his clothes back on, including the duster. It was cold outside, so it made sense; still, Auburn missed seeing what was underneath the long coat.

"Hey," she said, "I owe you an apology."

He looked at her. "Why?"

"Because I've been rude. I said things I shouldn't have."

He shook his head. "I offer the same apology to you."

"Okay." She took a deep breath. "Flip you for the bed."

His brows shot up. "I'll take the roll-up bed."

"You and Rose might be more comfortable in the king."

He kissed the baby's cheek. "We're comfortable anywhere together. Aren't we, pumpkin?"

Auburn's heart shifted. "You're getting very attached to her."

He nuzzled her cheek. "She's lured me in."

Auburn turned away. "Are you ready to turn in? Or are you a night owl?"

"We're both ready."

Auburn helped him pull the rollaway apart, straightened the sheets. He and the baby lay down on it, facing each other. Slowly, he ran a soothing palm over the child, and Rose relaxed.

"This is silly," Auburn said, looking at his boots hanging off the end, and hearing the springs creak. "We'll all sleep in the king. There's plenty of room. Rose in the middle."

He raised his head. "I don't need to keep that close of an eye on you."

She rolled her eyes and jerked his pillow from under his head. "I'll sleep better knowing you're not going to squash Rose by rolling over on her in that small bed."

He followed his pillow, which she'd tossed on the far

side of the bed. "Baby in between," she said, and he complied. "See? We're as far apart as California from Tennessee."

"It's still not proper," he hedged. "Ladies don't sleep in a bed with a man they don't know."

"Don't you worry about that," Auburn said, snuggling down on her side, grateful for the soft pillows and warm blanket. "I won't tell on Rose if you don't."

She leaned over and gave Rose a tiny kiss on the forehead, just to feel the satin of baby skin under her lips. Just once.

And then she realized how hard it would be to say goodbye when it was time for Rose and her cowboy to go back to wherever it was that they came from.

Closing her eyes, Auburn listened to Dillinger breathing deeply, unable to sleep herself. She was taunted by one nagging question: what would it feel like to sleep all night in such a drop-dead-sexy man's arms?

Divine, probably. Sinfully divine.

Chapter Seven

Auburn was pretending that she was asleep, but Dillinger knew she wasn't. He certainly couldn't sleep. His thoughts kept running around Auburn's incredible description of his home, and his wife. How could she have seen it so clearly, described it so well? The fact that she had spooked him, made him crazy. She claimed she had nothing to do with his appearance in this time and realm, and yet she knew all about his life.

The baby slept between them, content now. She wouldn't awaken for a feeding for a bit. He should sleep.

But sleep wouldn't come.

"Hey," a voice whispered in the darkness. He automatically stiffened, not certain he was ready to talk.

"What?"

"How old do you think Rose is?"

He had no idea. "About three months, maybe."

"That's what I was thinking."

"Why are you thinking about her age?"

He felt Auburn shift in the bed. There seemed to be miles between them, and yet not enough distance.

"I can't imagine a person leaving such a small baby on a porch step in bitter cold and snow."

Goose bumps ran over his skin. What if he hadn't opened the door? "I try not to think about some poor soul being that desperate. When I get back, I'll try to figure out who her mother is, see if I can help in some way." He had no idea how he would do that, but he could try.

"Wasn't there a church in town where she could have been left?"

"It's very far from my ranch. Whoever it was had to have been on foot. I didn't hear horses or any type of sleigh. Of course, I wasn't really listening. Rose was wailing, and I picked her up—and then I was here."

"Weren't you scared?"

"It happened too fast." Of course he'd been scared, totally panicked about being left with an infant.

"What did it feel like?" Auburn asked, her voice soft. "Traveling through time?"

He sat up, looked over at her in the darkness. "You really do believe me now, don't you?"

"Yes. I do. As crazy as I must be, I know you're telling the truth."

He sighed, relieved. "It felt like wind was tearing at every piece of me, and yet I felt no pain. I held the baby tight, and it seemed only a second passed before I was at your Six Flags." He frowned. "Why were you working there, anyway? You clearly have enough money for your needs."

"It's an adventure. All my life I wondered what was outside of my world. People always seemed like they were having so much fun at places like Disney World and Six Flags. I admired actors and actresses in stage plays, musicians in orchestras. I could never do any of those things, so I wanted to know. And I liked dressing up for a few hours and being someone else."

"You don't like your family? Your life?"

"I do," she said carefully, "but I need to rethink it."

"How much longer will you rethink?"

"Once Christmas is past, I'll probably go home."

He heard the hesitation in her voice and wondered. "I'm sure your parents are worried."

"I call them every once in a while. The conversation is short, but they know I'm safe."

"Will they be all right?"

"Yes. Apparently, my ex-fiancé still thinks I'll come to my senses and return to him, so he's not asking my parents to pay back any of the loans he's carrying for them." She let out a long sigh, and Dillinger could feel her worry for her family. "Banks aren't loaning money for anything. I suppose my folks had nowhere else to turn. But I got angry when I realized they felt me marrying him was good for their business relationship. It just didn't feel right. Not when you think you're marrying for love."

So she'd been in love with him. Something strange and unfamiliar smote Dillinger, making him question his feelings about this woman with whom he had nothing in common. Why would he be anguished that she'd had her heart broken? Had he hoped she'd been marrying for money, as she seemed to think her parents wanted? It wasn't the first time people would marry for financial considerations; it happened all the time, in every century. He doubted this era was any different than others.

"I'm sorry," he finally murmured, not knowing what else to say.

"Don't be," Auburn replied. "I'm in a better place now. Good night."

And that was all she intended to say on the matter, he realized. He admired her spunk, her sense of adventure. If he had to rely on a woman to help him, he was glad it was Auburn. She was kind and caring, and if she was a little unusual, it was probably because women were a bit different in this time.

He didn't like knowing so little about her, though, when she'd seen inside his home, his life and his marriage. She was still a stranger to him.

BRADLEY JACKSON DIDN'T like anyone making a fool of him, and his fiancée leaving right before their wedding had humiliated him. He didn't love Auburn, but he'd believed he was getting a good deal with her. Their marriage would be one of mutual respect—or so he'd thought.

Clearly, she hadn't respected him very much. There was only one way to save face, something very important to him, not just for his own name, but for the reputation of McGinnis Perfumes. He intended to explain that just as soon as he caught up to her, which wouldn't take long, thanks to excellent private investigators. And when he found her, he was going to spell out in language she couldn't misunderstand just what would happen to her company if she didn't return. And then let everyone know she'd gotten a case of cold feet, which would by then be hot to trot right up to the altar.

She owed him that much. She owed him a lot more, but making her understand her end of the business transaction was important to Bradley.

It was easy to get the information he needed from the security guard at the penthouse where she'd stayed—a dreadful, run-down place, in his opinion. But thankfully not so run-down that they didn't take credit cards, which his P.I. had traced.

"She was with a man and a baby," the guard told him after Bradley gave him a crisp hundred-dollar bill. Blood boiling at the thought that Auburn might have jilted him for another man, he decided he would be more than happy to ruin the company if she didn't play his way, and fast. He headed west, because the guard thought he'd heard something said about Christy River, which would be a stupid place for her to go. There'd be nothing for the citified, globe-trotting Auburn McGinnis in a two-bit town. A McGinnis should only be seen in the best places, such as Aspen and Dubai. He hoped she remembered who she was while she was sightseeing all over Texas, clearly not thinking about what she'd put him through.

What if she'd planned all this? The job at Six Flags—which horrified him—and the road-tripping with another man? Bradley would kill him, plain and simple. He doubted straitlaced Auburn would pick up a stranger, so it had to be someone she knew. Clearly someone who was married and who had a child, which necessitated the running and hiding.

And which also meant she was probably sleeping with the stranger, something she'd never done with Bradley. He would kill her because she'd made him wait while he was playing the diligent, if not entirely faithful, suitor.

Maybe he would hire some of his thugs to dispose of them neatly. The trail would have grown cold by the time the McGinnis family decided to send their own team of private investigators to look for their daughter, and to be brutally honest, the McGinnises didn't have that much money left.

Bradley would kill her if he caught her with another man. Especially a man with a baby, if the security guard had been right. Because Auburn had always told Bradley—insisted, even—that she never, ever wanted children.

Surely she didn't think she could pull a trick on him the size of Texas and expect not to pay dearly.

These were his fantasies, though he knew he'd never really harm her or anyone else. But it hurt like hell to get jilted by a woman who owed him big-time.

"THERE HAS TO BE A way to get you home," Auburn whispered so they wouldn't awaken Rose, whom they'd just fed and soothed back to sleep. The three of them lay in the dark, and the only one slumbering away was the baby. Auburn's mind was running in circles, and she wasn't certain if it was because she couldn't stop thinking about how warm and comforting it would be to snuggle up to Dillinger, or because sudden nerves that she couldn't explain had swept over her.

She was jumpy in the worst way.

"I can't imagine what brought me here in the first place," he replied, his voice deep and husky in the darkness. They'd quickly discovered that once Rose was asleep, nothing disturbed her. "If I can figure that out, I'll do everything in my power to reverse whatever happened, and hopefully get us back to Christmas River."

"You might send yourself further into the future. Or back to the time of pharaohs."

"That's a bit fanciful," Dillinger said.

"Why? How do you know this is where you were supposed to be in the first place?" She worked at the puzzle tenaciously, her nerves making her restless enough to pull apart a Rubik's cube. "There was a television show called—"

"Television show?"

She blinked. He would really freak when she turned on a television set for him. As overwhelmed as he was by automobiles, airplanes and highway traffic, he'd probably be fascinated by a TV. All men were. Then again, maybe she wouldn't introduce him to that particular pleasure just yet, Auburn thought with a giggle.

"What's so funny?"

"Nothing," she said. "A television show is like a stage show, but in a box. Did you see that box in the cabinet?"

"Yes."

"It plays pictures."

"How?"

"Beams and signals and things I'm not all that good at explaining. From a television station, they get sent all over the world, and are broadcast in homes where they have a television."

"So there are people in the boxes?"

"Pictures of people, really."

"And like those airplanes we saw, the people can get in them and go wherever they want."

She could feel his excitement, knew what he was asking. "But you can't travel through time in them, only across time zones, which is different."

"There's something here that will send us back," he insisted.

"I know," she said. "We'll figure it out."

She didn't know how. She sold perfume for a living; what did she know about time travel? She'd barely read any science fiction in school. "Maybe it was your thoughts that brought you forward?"

"Then I could think my way back? I doubt it. I'd already be home by now."

For some reason his words opened a painful place inside her. He wasn't ever going to stop thinking about the ranch where he'd lived with his wife. "Okay," she sighed, rolling over to look in his direction, even though she couldn't see him. "It all comes back to the baby, then."

"I don't see how a helpless baby can be responsible. She can't even speak."

"But you picked her up and found yourself here," Auburn pointed out.

"That's true."

Auburn reached out in the darkness to smooth a hand

over Rose's head, accidentally met Dillinger's hand doing the same. They both drew back instantly.

"Sorry," she murmured.

"Don't be. Maybe she's a good luck charm, and if we rub her the right way or often enough, she'll reveal the hidden passageway."

"Oh, wow," Auburn said, then laughed. "Who would have thought you'd have the gift of fantasy fiction inside you?"

"I told you," he said stiffly, "my wife read to me often. *Arabian Nights,* tales about the Knights of the Round Table…we had books in the nineteenth century, you know."

"I know," Auburn said. "It's just that you seem like such a tough guy to be interested in Arabian stories."

"I liked them very much, and Shakespeare, and anything we could find in the town library. *Arabian Nights* caused quite a sensation when it was translated into English just a few years ago."

She blinked. "Wasn't it older?"

"Of course. But the English translation was new."

She thought about stories and magic carpets and jumbo jets, and wondered how she could help him.

"So about this television show you were going to tell me about—"

"Never mind." She shook her head. "It was just a story, like those in *Arabian Nights.* It won't help us."

"Anything's possible," he said. "The fairy tales I plan to read to Rose will always have a happy ending."

"Those involve kissing, usually," Auburn said, "and a kiss didn't bring you here, so a kiss won't send you back."

He laughed. "That's funny."

"What? Kissing to make you travel through time?"

"Yes."

"Maybe. Kissing Rose hasn't exactly worked for you."

"No, but I like it. She's a sweet baby."

"I still think she's the charm." Auburn stared up at the ceiling in the dark, wondering about how charming and magical it would be to kiss the cowboy.

Suddenly, she sat up. "It's the earring!"

"What?"

"I saw your home when I held the earring. The earring is the key!"

"Not possible. I know for certain it wasn't a magical earring. I bought it in a store in California. Nothing unusual or fantastic about it. Just a guy going into a store to buy something for his wife."

"Still, go get it."

"No, thanks," he said. "I told you, I don't believe in magic."

"Time travel's not magical?"

"Look, an earring is no more magical than a kiss. It's all fairy tales."

She wrinkled her nose. They didn't have the first

clue about how to send him back. Maybe he was meant to stay here forever. "A kiss always worked in the fairy tale. Some people think they're powerful in real life."

"I'll show you that a kiss isn't magical outside of books," he offered, "if you must be convinced."

"All right," she said with a put-upon sigh, "make it a fast one, though." Of course she was fibbing—she was dying to do more than a drive-by on Dillinger's chiseled lips—but for the sake of modesty she had to act as though she was doing him a huge favor. "I'll be very disappointed when nothing happens, though."

"So will I. It'll mean I'm kissing the wrong woman."

She was about to try to come up with a return zinger when she felt his lips cover hers in the most hot, possessive way she could have imagined. The baby between them didn't move, but everything inside Auburn moved like crazy, and then she heard a howling wind, felt herself being thrown into Dillinger's arms.

When Auburn awakened, she was very, very cold.

She sat up. Rose was between them, sleeping peacefully. The soft blankets were gone, and so was the Hilton hotel room.

Dillinger sat up, too, turned on a gas lamp on a table next to him. He stared at her, his dark blue eyes angry.

"Who the *hell* are you?" he demanded.

Chapter Eight

Auburn jumped from the bed, looked wildly around the room. It was smallish and spare, with just a spindle bed and two plain nightstands for furniture, the walls a rough-hewn wood. Her clothes were the same as she'd been wearing, a pair of comfortable Victoria's Secret sweats and a soft pink fleece shirt. She had on the same half-bootie Uggs she'd lain down on the bed with, not feeling comfortable stripping with a man she barely knew, and not knowing when she'd have to jump from bed in the night to help with Rose.

Dillinger, on the other hand, was shirtless now, and maybe more considering he was covered with a sheet. And he looked oh so achingly beautiful. But she didn't want to be in a weird place with him gazing at her strangely, even if it meant possibly getting to see him in the buff. "Blast!"

His face held annoyance, but zero recognition. "Why are you in my house?"

Dear God, please tell me I'm not in 1892! "Where am I?"

"Get out," Dillinger said. *"Now."*

"Oh, my goodness," Auburn said. "Dillinger, please!"

He frowned. "How do you know my name?"

"Because I— Because you brought me here!"

"I assure you I did not."

That kiss was turning into the worst idea she'd ever had, even worse than thinking she should marry Bradley, which had been dumb in retrospect, but now seemed fairly harmless in her gallery of bad decisions. "Dillinger, you were in Texas with me, in the twenty-first century. My name is Auburn McGinnis. We kissed, and somehow ended up back in your house. Don't you remember?"

"I know I was sound asleep until you shrieked. Good thing you didn't wake the baby. She's a light sleeper."

Auburn gasped. "Light sleeper! Rose has been sleeping like a rock ever since I met you."

He got out of bed, long and lean and yet muscled from hard work. And he wasn't nude; he had on a pair of long johns that did nothing to hide the strength and form of well-developed legs. Auburn didn't have time to admire the scenery. "You can't throw me out. I can tell it's cold outside." There was clearly no central heating in the house, which meant it was even colder outside.

He eyed her, frowning at her sweats. She glanced down to see what had caught his gaze, realized the sequined peace sign on the side of her leg must seem very odd to him. "Look, I helped you in my century, so you can't toss me out on my backside."

"I don't take in gypsies. But you can sleep in the rocking chair next to the fireplace until morning," he said begrudgingly.

"Oh, thanks," she snapped, thinking of her penthouse apartment and the Hilton bed she'd shared with him. "Your generosity must be legendary." Why had she ever thought kissing him would be such a swell idea? A few seconds of pleasure, and she'd landed in cold hell. "What's the temperature outside, anyway?"

"Probably somewhere around ten degrees, which is the only reason I'm not booting you out. That, and the fact that snow is up to the windows. You'd never make it in those— In what you're wearing." He cocked a rifle, laid it by the bed. "Think twice before you come back into my bedroom."

"Are you insane?" she demanded, gasping.

"No. Just don't plan to have a thief stealing from me."

She blinked. "I have no reason to steal anything. I have plenty of money." She reached for her Louis Vuitton bag to show him and groaned. Of course *that* hadn't made the little time jaunt with her. She was penniless, had no documents to prove who she was or where she was from, and the cause of her dilemma intended to kick her out in the morning.

With a glare at the man she was beginning to wish she'd never met, Auburn stalked off toward the den and the rocking chair next to a nearly burned out fire in the stone fireplace.

Funny how it had all looked so cozy when she'd seen him sitting here with Polly. At the moment, it looked anything but cozy, and Auburn was none too happy about it as she tried to get comfortable in surely the stiffest rocking chair ever put on earth.

DILLINGER UNCOCKED THE RIFLE, but kept it near the bed. The woman in rags clearly had no place to go, but how dare she sneak into his house? He might have shot her, and no one could blame him.

They *would,* of course, blame him, based on his reputation, but that was the life of a gunslinger. He checked Rose, a smile coming to his face. She was sleeping like an angel, and he almost hoped he didn't find her mother anytime soon.

His brow knitted. Unless the unhinged woman in the other room was her mother. Surely she hadn't left her baby on his porch, then sneaked back in to get her. They looked nothing alike. Rose was blonde and delicate, the whiskey-haired woman somewhat coarse and yet not unattractive in her own way, if her hair weren't so wild.

He'd never seen such unkempt curls, as if she'd been blowing across the Texas desert, tumbleweed-style. He preferred straight hair. Polly had possessed hair of the glossiest ebony, beautiful when light shone on it.

Dillinger got back into bed, snuggled up next to the baby to keep her warm, and tried not think about the poor woman sleeping in the next room, and how she'd pretended to have kissed him in another time.

As if he'd believe such a mad fairy tale.

WITH AUBURN'S LOVE OF four- and five-star hotels, it really wasn't that difficult to find her rose convertible Mercedes parked outside the only decent hotel on the highway. Bradley had no idea why she would be traveling along such an ugly, barren road; there were certainly no signs of city sophistication around. He hated it here.

The obvious answer was that she'd thought he'd never look for her in a backwater like this. She was clearly bent on avoiding him at all costs, a fact that stung his already wounded pride. No doubt she didn't want to be caught with her married boyfriend.

She was busted now.

Bradley went inside, explained to the young and inexperienced desk clerk that he'd forgotten his key. She asked for his name and he started talking about his wife and their baby—his wife had wonderful whiskey-colored hair and was so petite he had to order her clothes—and they were traveling with her brother in that custom-painted rose-red Mercedes out front.

He could tell the clerk knew exactly who he was talking about, so he slipped her a hundred dollars to encourage her to bend the rules and give him a pass card to Auburn's room. His blood ran a bit cold at the thought of what he might find there, preparing himself for the sight of a naked Auburn in another man's arms. Bradley was afraid he might kill them, but of course, there was no reason to do that. Calling the loans on her company would be enough to destroy her emotionally, a much more satisfying revenge.

Quietly, he stuck the card in the keypad, swiped it. No sound of concern came from the other side, so they hadn't heard him. With a triumphant shove he flung open the door.

The room was empty. He let out a sigh of disappointment and walked inside. The bed was made, a rollaway folded up. Auburn's clothes were there, as well as a bag of Pampers and some baby formula, and her Louis Vuitton purse, which she'd bought in Paris. He couldn't imagine why she'd leave without her purse, and decided maybe she'd gone for a walk. Maybe the baby had needed soothing.

A golden earring lay on the floor. He picked it up, admired the tiny bells connected to a fishhook-style wire.

Pretty, but not something he would have imagined

Auburn wearing. She tended to stick to demure pearl studs. But maybe it was a gift from her traveling companion, a thought that made Bradley's blood freeze.

Maybe he hadn't known Auburn as well as he thought he had.

He sat down on the bed to wait.

"EXCUSE ME," AUBURN said to the grouchy male who walked into the den with the baby against his wonderfully wide chest, "can you tell me where the bathroom is?" Her bladder was complaining bitterly, but she hadn't dared awaken the grouch to ask him the location of his potty.

He glowered at her, his black brows lowered. "I assume you mean the outhouse."

"Outhouse? In ten degree weather? You're kidding, right?"

He crouched in front of the fire with the baby, reaching to stir the embers with an iron poker. She gasped, snatching Rose from him. "You don't stoke a fire with a baby in your arms. What if a spark jumped out and hit her?"

He grunted, which she took for unwilling agreement, and threw a couple of logs onto the fire. It would have been a pleasure watching his back muscles ripple and his trim waist flex if she hadn't been so annoyed.

"Have you changed the baby yet?"

"I just awoke. And you're not going to be here long enough to worry about drying the baby."

Rose had other ideas, setting up a din loud enough to shake the rafters. "Oh," Auburn said, her tone sweet, "here's your baby back."

He tried feeding the child, which worked for a while, and Auburn fumbled with the fire, doing her best to imitate what she'd seen the cowboy do, while he sat in the other rocker, trying to calm his angel. He got a rather unsatisfactory burp from Rose, then started pacing with her, his steps growing more frantic as the baby's wails became louder.

"I don't know what she wants," Dillinger finally said.

"Well, I know I need to use a ladies' room," Auburn reminded him, "and I'll bet she wants her diaper changed. We women tend to feel very irritated when things aren't going well for us in that department."

"There's a chamber pot in the guest room you can use," he finally said, looking panicked.

A chamber pot? If she was in 1892, and there was no reason at this point to think she wasn't, indoor plumbing on a remote ranch wasn't an option. "Thank you," she said. "I'll be right back and then I'll help you with Rose."

He didn't say anything, but his eyes communicated that she should hurry. Auburn smiled and went to find the guest room. A chamber pot was there, as well as a washbowl on a wooden stand. She wondered what she'd do with the pot once she finished, decided she'd dump it out the window for the sake of cleanliness. It was only pee, right? "I'll deal with the other track later," she muttered, "once I figure out the dreaded chamber pot."

Five minutes later, she went back into the main room, where Rose was still sobbing her eyes out. "I wonder if you've got a stuck bubble or a gas pain," Auburn murmured, taking her from Dillinger, who seemed relieved. "Did you change her?"

"Not yet." He looked a bit worried. "I don't have any diapers."

"We had Pampers— Oh, that's right." Auburn glanced around. "And since the baby was left on your porch—that's still the story, right? It hasn't changed now that we're here and you seem to have developed convenient amnesia where I'm concerned?"

"Right," he said, with a growl that conveyed his irritation. "I found her on my porch yesterday. I would have taken her to town to see if anyone knew whose baby she is, but as you can see by looking out the window, the snowfall would impede any progress past the front door. I could make it to the forest if I had to, but it would be hard work."

Snow was banked up to the windowsill and flurries continued to drift down from the sky. "Well, get a sheet, then," Auburn said. "We'll just have to be creative."

He went to do as she asked. "Now cut it into diaper-size rectangles. Just cut one, and let's see how we do with it. We may need to rethink our pattern."

She gently laid Rose on the rag rug in front of the fire. "Just a minute, sweetie, your cowboy is going to make you a wonderful little diaper, and once you're clean, you're going to be so happy."

"I hope so," Dillinger said, handing her a decent-looking rectangle, even if there were some ragged edges.

"I hope you have pins," Auburn said, and he went to take some from what looked like a sewing box. It was probably Polly's, and Auburn made a note to dig through that later for more information on how a woman survived in these conditions. She pulled up Rose's little nightgown. "See?" She pointed to the baby's bottom. "A Pamper!"

He came close to look. "A tiny girdle," he said, his voice amazed. "Where can we buy those?"

"You can buy them in the twenty-first century, but not here," Auburn replied. "They haven't been invented yet. This proves you were with me in my century!"

He looked at her. "It doesn't prove that. There's no such thing as time travel. It's a tale, just like in all those books." He pointed to his impressive collection of leather-bound books on a ledge near the fireplace: Shakespeare, *One Thousand and One Arabian Nights, King Arthur and the Knights of the Round Table* and many others, just as he'd described.

"Where's Polly's earring?" Auburn demanded.

"On the desk," Dillinger said, watching her wrap Rose in the diaper. "How do you know about my wife?"

"You told me." She glanced toward the writing stand. "And there's only one earring on the desk, just as we both knew."

"We did?" he asked, frowning again. "Did you take the other one?"

"No, I didn't." Auburn sighed and raised the baby to her chest after she was satisfied with her diaper job. "It's in your duster pocket, as it was in the future."

Looking at her as if she had two heads—and she was feeling as if she did by now, and maybe three—he went to check his duster. He sent a suspicious look Auburn's way. "There's nothing here. You must have stolen the other earring to convince me of your story."

"Oh, holy smokes!" Auburn got up, handed Rose to him and headed toward the front door. "I've had enough of you to last me for three centuries."

"Where are you going?" Dillinger demanded, following her. "You won't make it past the forest edge."

"Trust me, cowboy, I'll be fine. I'm from New York, remember? This isn't the first time I've seen snow."

"It's ten miles to town," he warned.

"I'll have really awesome glutes by the time I get there then," she retorted.

He sighed. "I don't like opinionated women."

"I don't like men who are jerks and who accuse me of stealing!"

He took a long look at her face, studying her. "You can stay until the snow clears enough for me to take you to town in the sleigh," Dillinger finally said, "if you mind the baby."

Auburn blinked. "You want me to be your babysitter?"

"I think I can trust you to have Rose's best interests at heart," he said slowly. "Although I don't want you getting in my bed again, no matter if it drops below zero outside. Sharing body warmth isn't done between strangers, at least not in this house."

"Don't worry, buster," Auburn snapped, "there isn't a fairy tale written that could convince me to sleep in the bed of a true warlock."

He scowled at that. "You may use the guest room."

"You are generous indeed, my knight in shining armor."

"I prefer a more dulcet tone when being spoken to," he said, and Auburn just laughed. He didn't know how lucky he was that she hadn't beaned him with that fireplace poker—an idea she hadn't completely abandoned.

Chapter Nine

Something about the woman's story niggled at him, though Dillinger couldn't say exactly what. She bothered him, for one thing, probably since he was used to being alone. And she was noisy, always humming, which was going to irritate him with the three of them shut up in the house. But the baby seemed to like it, so he didn't voice any complaint. The woman kept to herself, and though he'd kept a careful eye on her at first, she'd gone about the business of feeding, rocking and playing with the baby. She'd come up with a unique system of triple-wrapping Rose's diaper so nothing flooded out inconveniently, and cut down one of his undershirts to make a tiny nightgown for the little one. When she'd used Polly's sewing box, he'd started to protest, then asked himself why it mattered as long as she was tending the child.

He had no idea how he'd ended up with a baby and a woman in his house in the space of twenty-four hours or so. He who had been a loner for a year, an outcast, was suddenly a family man of sorts.

It was a lot to take in.

"What's for dinner?" Auburn asked, and he started, not expecting her to address him. She'd kept a huffy lock on her lips around him, which somehow aggravated Dillinger, since he knew she was doing it on purpose.

"I could try to shoot a rabbit or a duck, although in this snowstorm, I think all game will be hard to find. There's a storeroom in the attic with cured meat, and some preserves I bought in town belowstairs."

"Sounds like dinner at the Four Seasons," Auburn said with a sigh. "What about formula for Rose?"

"I milk the cows twice a day," Dillinger said, "and she drinks milk just fine."

"Does dinner fall under my job description or yours?" Auburn asked, and he looked at her.

"You just take care of Rose, and I'll tend to the fire and the meals. This storm should blow over in a week."

"A week!"

He turned to look at her, surprised she didn't know. "You said you'd seen snow. Sometimes bad weather comes in and stays. Happens every winter."

"Yes, but…okay." She sighed again. "When do you start getting ready for Christmas? Or do you?"

He didn't. Polly had taken such joy in preparing for the holiday that he hadn't had the stomach for it now that she was gone. "You can make a meat pie, if you wish, to celebrate the season."

Auburn sat in the rocker, contentedly rocking Rose, who was much more content now that the adults were calm. "I don't know how to make a meat pie."

"You don't?"

"Don't make it sound like my education has been neglected," she told him. "I can make a heckuva chocolate pie with Jell-O pudding."

"Jell-O?"

"Oh, never mind." She shook her head. "I so wish I had my Louis Vuitton bag. Or something of my own. It feels so strange not to even have the hairbrush I like. I bought it at a salon in Beverly Hills. There was a hairdresser there who was extremely popular. His name was Jose, and you can't believe how marvelous—"

She caught the expression of disbelief Dillinger knew was written on his face, closed her eyes and rocked the baby without saying anything else. Such tales she told! Surely she knew he didn't believe any of her yarns. But maybe she was like Scheherazade, with a thousand wild tales to tell. He liked to be read to; he loved stories. Maybe he should encourage her storytelling. It was what gypsies did best, after all.

"Go on," he said, making himself sound interested.

She looked at him suspiciously. "Why?"

"I enjoy stories."

"You have a pretty good one to tell yourself."

He glowered. "What does that mean?"

"You know, the reformed gunslinger bit. The magic earrings. The baby on the porch. You won't remember this, but you can fly through the air. All in all, you're not the most boring guy I ever met."

He wished he hadn't asked. She was gifted in fibs and outlandish nonsense, and clearly planned not to miss an opportunity to try to convince him he'd gone snow mad. It happened to some people and even he was a little tense during the long months of winter. But that was only since Polly had died.

He just dreaded being lonely.

"I'm going to chop some wood and milk the cows," he said.

"Fine," she replied in a tone that implied *good riddance*.

Ungrateful termagant. He knew one more lie she'd told: he had never, ever kissed that surly woman.

He'd considered whether he had, once she'd mentioned it, simply because it was so implausible. She had full, bow-shaped lips that might be good to kiss, if a man liked quarrelsome females. He did not. Luckily, the one-second image he'd had of kissing those lips wouldn't reappear in his head; he didn't know her, and the thought would never cross his mind.

Again, anyway.

AFTER TWO HOURS, when he could tell that she had no plan to talk to him after the unpleasant way he was treating her, the big lug finally decided to break the silence.

"I'll hold the baby now," he said, "if you want to cook the meal."

"Can't refuse that offer." Auburn rose, curious to see what was "belowstairs" and what was in the attic. It wasn't going to be like dining at Delmonico's or even fast food, but surely he had some decent provisions put back.

The belowstairs pantry was a wonderland, given she'd expected to find a few cobwebs and maybe some pickled pig's feet. He'd stocked up on glass jars of items he'd bought in town, which were all nicely labeled. She grabbed a jar of pickled asparagus and some apple-sauce, put it in the kitchen, and headed up to the attic by way of a small ladder. Okay, it wasn't shopping at the grocery, with everything in nice small chunks and wrapped in cellophane, but there was enough meat up here to last Dillinger through the winter. There was even some smoked salmon. She grabbed that and went back down the ladder, closing the loft after herself.

"This won't be terrible," she told him. "Now all we need is some beer."

"Ale?" He frowned. "Women do not drink."

"This one does. Where's the stash? I didn't see that in the attic."

He shook his head. "It's outside the back door in the barrel."

She grabbed two mugs and went to fetch the "ale." It was bottled, she was surprised to see. Snatching up two bottles, she went inside and handed one to Dillinger, who accepted it with resignation.

"I suppose I have nothing to hide," he said, "and no one to care, but I never thought I'd have house help that tipples."

"If you want dinner, you'll leave me to drink mine in peace." It wasn't Corona with a lime, but it wasn't milk from old Bessie outside, either, so she opened it with pleasure. Then she turned her attention to figuring out Dillinger's kitchen, which was rudimentary to a woman who'd spent her life admiring copper pots and fancy stoves in gourmet kitchens. "Julia Child would have a fit," she murmured.

Dillinger called, "Did you say something?"

"No." Auburn decided to serve the asparagus and the applesauce cold. She cut some generous chunks of bread, laid the salmon on a white plate and slapped it all on the table. "Dinner is served."

"That's it?"

She shrugged. "Looks awesome to me."

He wore an expression of disappointment.

"I'll get better," she promised. "You said I have maybe a week of being stuck in this igloo to figure it out."

"All right," he said grudgingly. "I can't imagine why your mother didn't teach you how to cook. All girls of marriageable age know how to prepare a proper meal. It's important on the range. Rose will know how to serve many dishes that will please her husband."

"I'd take offense at that, but I'm too hungry." Auburn sat down at the table, said a fast grace, which seemed to surprise him, and dug in. Rose lay on a soft fur pallet a few feet away from the fireplace, where they could keep an eye on her and make sure she stayed warm.

"What do you do around here for pleasure?" Auburn asked. "I'd go stark mad without a television or a radio to listen to."

He frowned. "Don't know what that is, but as I said, I read a lot. I do some woodwork. I'll do a few house projects while the snow is high. It's a good time to do things I'm normally too busy on the ranch to get to."

"But you have no family? No friends?" Auburn asked, biting into the dark brown bread. It wasn't San Francisco sourdough, but it wasn't bad, either.

"No."

"Do you not need human companionship?" Auburn thought no man could—or should—be an island, especially one who had to live in such outcast conditions.

He drank his beer. Looked at her for a second, then said, "No."

She shook her head. "Have any cards?"

"Playing cards is—"

"I'm sure it is. We're ten miles from civilization, and that would take a day by foot, probably."

"Only a couple hours by buggy in the springtime," Dillinger said helpfully.

"So I don't think anyone cares whether we play cards, do you?"

He put down his bread. "You're a very odd woman."

"When you were in my century, I thought you were the oddest man I'd ever met."

He seemed to consider that. "Back to your question about Christmas—"

"We always had a turkey. I don't think I'm too much on meat pies," she said.

He had no comment, so they ate in silence. It wasn't bad as far as food went, better than McDonald's or Lean Cuisine, and yet not Wolfgang Puck.

"I'm going out for a while," Dillinger said, "before the light fades, which it will do early. Will you be all right with Rose?"

"Of course," Auburn said, not exactly unhappy about a chance to snoop around his house without him watching her like a hawk. He probably had to check on his cattle—he'd mentioned he had some— or whatever else needed to be tended to on a ranch. "We'll be fine."

"Good." He stood, put down his cloth napkin on

the table. "Thank you for the meal. It was nice to have…to have."

He'd been going to say *have one prepared for me,* but stopped himself. She wondered why. "You're welcome. Thank you for sharing your food. It was surprisingly good."

He blinked. Then nodded, wrapped himself in his coat and a scarf and a well-worn western hat, grabbed his rifle and left. Auburn cleaned the kitchen, carefully going through the cabinets and drawers to see what utensils he had that she could use to better cook the next meal. She checked on Rose constantly, her ear tuned for the slightest noise, but the baby seemed happy for the moment.

Auburn couldn't restrain herself another second.

She crept over to the writing desk, hoping Dillinger didn't look through any of the windows and see her, because he'd never stop harping about her being a thief if he did. Polly's earring lay there; she wondered where the other earring was. She was dying to pick it up, but was afraid to—she'd been holding one of the earrings when she'd seen this house, and Dillinger. He hadn't always been a lonely man. Once upon a time he'd been a very happy husband.

A framed charcoal drawing of a beautiful woman sat near the earring. With trepidation, Auburn picked it up, knowing she was looking at Polly. She'd seen her in the vision she'd had; this was a pretty true rendering.

"You must have loved him so much," she told the drawing. Obviously Polly had or she wouldn't still be trying to help him. That was the only conclusion Auburn could come to—Polly knew how lonely her husband had to be. It made sense. There was a baby now in his life, and a woman…. "Although he treats me like house help," Auburn said, "so I don't know if that's what you had in mind or not. But I hate to tell you, girlfriend, I'm not going to be able to stay here. It's too different. I'm a city girl, born and bred. You'll need a replacement when I figure out how to get back home. Not that he doesn't have his really fine points, but if you were looking for someone for him to hang out with, I'm not your girl."

She put the picture back down, glanced out the window. Nervousness crept over her as she saw the darkening sky. Surely Dillinger wouldn't leave her here alone after dark. She was okay with a few daylight hours of solitude, but really she wasn't made for nighttime seclusion in these unknown surroundings.

"He doesn't have enough beer for me to hold out in this fort for an entire winter," she softly told the sleeping Rose. "So if I can't figure out how to get home, we're going to have to convince him to start a home microbrewery."

Suddenly a gunshot rang out, the echo reverberating from the surrounding forest. Auburn jumped to the window, tried to peer through the darkness. She couldn't see anything past the frost on the panes. "Oh, no, please, no," she murmured, panic spreading through her. He said he had no friends, said he was a reformed gunslinger. He had enemies. What if someone had shot him? What if he'd accidentally shot himself? What if he was out there somewhere, bleeding in the snow, freezing to death in the forest that surrounded the ranch except for the road he'd cleared to town?

"What if I'm stuck in this century forever by myself with an abandoned baby?" she said with a gasp, feeling herself hyperventilate, wondering if Dillinger had a paper bag somewhere. Did they make paper bags in 1892? Should she shove her head between her knees or was that for a bloody nose?

She heard footsteps and the sound of boots scraping on the porch. Surely that was Dillinger! Did she dare open the door? Were there bandits out here, or even hungry Indians, like she'd read about in books? Every Native American she'd ever met had been warm and friendly, but this was 1892; wasn't this the century of Jesse James and the Dalton Gang and anyone who wanted to settle a score with a gun?

She grabbed a frying pan for protection and waited breathlessly at the door. It suddenly burst open and a dripping, bloody mess of feathers was thrust in her face.

Auburn screamed.

Dillinger looked at her over the bird's feet. "Here," he said gruffly, "this is for you."

Auburn stared at the huge dead bird, realizing Dillinger was making some kind of peace offering. "Oh, you *shouldn't* have!" she exclaimed, her heart thundering. *And I really mean that!*

"You won't want the frying pan for a turkey," he said in a patient tone. "We can roast it in the stove once you've plucked the feathers, and eat it for an early Christmas meal."

"I— Pluck?" She put a hand over her jumping heart. She didn't even pluck her own eyebrows; the nice, efficient cosmetician at Elizabeth Arden Red Door Spa took care of waxing and plucking and all that jazz.

He gestured with the bird, indicating she should take his trophy. "Oh, my," she said, feeling squeamish. "Dillinger, if you don't mind, uh—"

"You don't know how to clean a turkey, do you?" He regarded her sorrowfully, disappointment clearly etched in his face.

She shook her head, trying not to be sick at the smell of dead wild turkey.

He sighed. "All right," he said. "You're more of a princess than help, but I suppose you're doing a pretty good job of taking care of Rose."

"Thank you for the turkey," she said in her meekest voice, not wanting to hurt his feelings. Clearly, he'd tried to please her, but darn it, dead bird just wasn't a rose-topped box of Godiva.

He nodded and disappeared with his prize. She could hear him crunching through the snow at the side of the house, heading toward the back, where he would now do heaven only knew what to that poor turkey. Rose awakened then, so Auburn went to get her and to figure out how to manage the double-ended banana-shaped glass bottle that served as the early precursor to Playtex plastic bottles.

"Come on, goddess of time travelers, send me back home," Auburn murmured, relaxing at the comforting scent of baby as she held Rose and made the bottle.

And that's when it hit her: a kiss had brought her here.

A kiss might send her back.

She had to figure out a way to get that cowboy to kiss her, although he'd sworn never to do it, swore he'd never done it in the first place.

But maybe a man who brought a woman a wild turkey had kissing on his mind.

Maybe.

Chapter Ten

After he finished cleaning the turkey and putting it away in the cold room, Dillinger went inside to find Auburn and Rose. They were on the fur rug together, staring up at the ceiling.

Auburn sat up. "It's a lovely turkey," she told him.

He shook his head at her squeamish expression. "You've never seen fresh game before, have you?"

"No, I haven't."

He sat down at the table, pulled out a knife and began whittling a block of wood.

"Tell me again how I ended up in the future with you." He couldn't quite believe her crazy story, but it was becoming quite obvious to him that this woman who could neither cook nor fend for herself on a range, and who dressed in clothes he'd never even seen on a beggar, although she seemed quite well fed and happy, wasn't from anyplace he'd been. He was reasonably well traveled, having spent much time on cattle drives across the States, and also taking a few trips to England and to Scotland to look at hardy cattle.

Auburn was like no one he'd ever met.

She sighed. "You landed in a stage show where I was performing. You were wearing your duster and had Rose in your arms. I thought you were a new extra who hadn't had time to find a babysitter. I took you home to help you out, but I knew something wasn't ordinary about you when you levitated off my sofa."

He looked into her big eyes, and saw that she believed she was telling the truth.

"And why don't I remember any of this?"

She shook her head. "I haven't figured that out. Maybe traveling back in time to where you belong erased your memory."

"But you recall everything."

"I don't belong here," she told him. "When you were in my century, you remembered everything about your life here."

"So if you don't belong here, and I don't belong there, have we been brought together for any type of…"

She looked at him. "Romantic reasons? No. I'd just broken off an engagement. It's not a good time for me to take up with another man. Also, you and I have nothing in common, as you've figured out by now."

"Was I as helpless in your century?"

She smiled. "More so. But you were trying to figure out how to manage a baby, too. I just have to figure out how to boil water without using a microwave."

"Microwave?"

"Never mind."

"So," he said with a sigh, wondering what this all meant, "why did it happen?"

"We thought it was the baby who brought us together, since you traveled forward when you picked her up off the porch. That was all we could think of at the time."

He considered Auburn's soft red-brown curls and her bow-shaped lips. "Did I accidentally land in the traveling show? Or was there a reason?"

"It wasn't a traveling show, it was just an amusement park. And I think it was random coincidence. There was no particular reason for you to travel there."

"Except for you."

She shook her head. "But anyone might have taken you home."

"Did anyone else notice me?"

She blinked. "I—I don't know. I called in my resignation that night, leaving a message for Harry that I had to quit. He left me a message in return that he'd forward my check wherever I wanted it to go. I gave him my parents' address, but he never mentioned anything about you at all." She frowned, looking at the baby. "Now that I think about it, none of the other performers seemed

particularly shocked that a man and a baby had suddenly
appeared onstage. The audience thought it was part of
the show, I guess."

"So it's possible that only you could see me."

"No, because the security guard saw you later on at
my penthouse." She shook her head. "It has nothing to
do with me. Like I said, random coincidence."

That didn't completely suit him. He liked the idea that
she'd been meant to find him. If that was the case, it
meant there was a reason for his traveling through time.

Yet he couldn't figure out the connection between
him and Auburn and the baby. "How do you get back?"

"I don't know," Auburn said, and gave an unexpected
sniffle. He was afraid she was about to cry, a horrifying
thought really, because she'd been calm up to now, and
he sensed that calm ebbing away.

"I miss my family," she said, wiping at her eyes. "I
know they made some mistakes, but it was only my intention to be gone a little while, let the air clear around
my wedding and the bad financial deals and everything.
And I know it's kind of cool with you to be out here, all
Lonesome Gunslinger on the Prairie, but I need people.
I want to be with my family at Christmas. Frankly, I'll
go mad if I have nothing to listen to out here but the
wind blowing."

He was stunned. It had never occurred to him that
maybe she was *stuck* here. "We'll figure something

out." One more thing was niggling at him. "About that kissing business—"

"Never mind about that," Auburn said. "Forget I mentioned it."

"Well, it would be hard for me to kiss a woman not my wife," he said, feeling he had to explain.

"Funny, you didn't mention that in my century."

"Well, we're here now. In my house."

In *her* house. The unspoken words hung between them. Auburn's eyes went wide, and he could tell she was surprised by his feelings. Maybe he was overly sentimental, but it hadn't been that long, only a year, since Polly had died. This still felt like her home. "I'm sorry," he said.

"Don't be," Auburn murmured. "I'd feel the same way about being married. Sort of too close to it."

He nodded. She looked so sweet and vulnerable right now and he tried not to think about kissing her. Then he wondered about holding her as a man held a woman…and then he made himself think about the turkey he'd just plucked and dressed, so he wouldn't think about Auburn in his arms anymore.

But she was beginning to play on his mind.

Like a wonderfully magical spell.

He had to send her back, though, if he could figure out a way to do it. After glancing at her as she gently picked Rose up from the fur rug so she could rock her, he went over to his bookshelf and thoughtfully considered every title on the ledge.

Then he chose a book of children's fairy tales and sat down to think.

BY DAY THREE AUBURN had figured out the outhouse—using it wasn't as bad as she'd expected, but it was certainly no picnic—learned how to take a bath and wash her hair, and snitched a pair of Dillinger's oldest jeans and a large flannel shirt so she could wash her clothes.

All in all, she was beginning to feel like a pioneer. The adventurous side of her, the side that wanted to drive across the United States, work at different places, meet different people while she recovered from her wedding meltdown, was feeling pretty satisfied. The only thing taking the bloom off her rose was that she couldn't call an end to this vacation and go home.

Her gaze found Dillinger as he took the turkey from the stove. It was perfectly roasted. He'd surrounded the bird with potatoes and some carrots. He'd stuffed it with an onion. The house smelled heavenly, but this didn't really feel like Christmas to Auburn. "Why are we celebrating the holiday early?"

"Who knows how long you'll be here?" Dillinger didn't look her way as he basted the turkey. "You could get whisked back any day now."

"I hope so."

"Then again, you might be here permanently."

She dreaded the thought, which loomed large and painful, and a distinct possibility.

Unless it was the baby.

"I've been thinking," Dillinger said. "I know I said I'd never kiss you, but if you want me to, I will."

Auburn shook her head. "I respect your feelings about your wife."

He winced. "It's not the same."

Auburn wasn't certain she liked that. "So you'd be the admirable prince doing his duty, and off I'd go?"

He shrugged, and stuffed the turkey back into the black iron stove.

"Maybe I'll just click my heels together three times, murmur 'There's no place like home,' and that would work, too."

"Sometimes I don't understand what you're talking about."

She wandered to the fireplace to look at the beautiful wooden cradle Dillinger had brought down from the attic. When she'd asked him where he'd gotten it, he hadn't answered. By the pained look on his face, she figured it had been planned for his and Polly's children.

Rose liked the cradle just fine. She slept in it in the guest room with Auburn, snug and warm. "How much longer until the snow clears, do you think?"

"Another day or so. If you want, I'll take you to town

in the buckboard so you can get some clothes. They won't have a lot of ready-made things, but perhaps some of the women can help you with something."

"Oh, no, thank you," Auburn said. She might have to live here a long time, and the last thing she wanted was people gossiping about her and Dillinger living together unmarried. In her time it wouldn't have mattered so much; in this era, it would.

"I feel stir-crazy," she murmured.

"You're homesick, not snow mad. It's normal," Dillinger told her. "Let's go outside."

"And leave the baby?"

"Oh." He closed the stove door and turned to look at her. "You're right. And I can't take her outside. I'd be too afraid of pneumonia."

"It's all right," Auburn said. "How are the fairy tales?"

"Well, they've made me think that you may be onto something about kissing. It can be a powerful talisman."

"Oh, I believe it," Auburn said, her spirits lifting at the thought of kissing him. It had to be the only way to get home. But she didn't want him to feel bad about it, as if he was dishonoring his wife in any way. Auburn had a funny feeling that if the kiss had negative vibes attached to it, it might backfire. "With my luck, I'd end up in ancient Egypt."

"I'm not that bad of a kisser!" Dillinger washed his hands in a bucket of water he'd warmed, dried them and said, "After our Christmas dinner, I suggest we experiment with your idea."

"All right." *Here's wishing on every lucky star in the universe that he's got the magic kiss.*

FROM THE EDGE OF the forest, Pierre could see smoke rising from the chimney of Dillinger's house. He was back. Pierre knew the gunslinger would return, but he hadn't expected company, which completely ruined Pierre's plans.

A woman walked outside, tossed water into the snow, went back in the house. Pierre held a spyglass up to his eye, trying to see who she might be. No one in town would come to visit Dillinger; Pierre had seen to the complete ruin of the scoundrel's reputation.

That meant he'd brought someone from outside Christmas River. It made Pierre even more angry. How dare Dillinger think he was going to go on and live his life as if Polly had never been in it?

If Dillinger thought he could replace her with another wife, Pierre would figure out a way to put a quick stop to that. His sister had never known happiness, and Dillinger would not know happiness, either. Pierre would wait until the rancher left the house, and pay a call on his visitor, find out what the gunslinger was up to.

If she was a woman brought to provide companionship for Dillinger Kent, she would quickly hear many reasons why she needed to pack up and go home as soon as the train tracks cleared.

If he had done the unthinkable and found himself a mail order bride, Dillinger would soon find himself a widower once again.

The thought made Pierre smile.

Chapter Eleven

"Dinner is served," Dillinger said. He was trying to be courtly, having learned something from the fairy tales he'd been consuming in his pursuit of a theory on how to send a princess back to wherever she belonged. Not that Auburn acted like a princess. He felt bad that he'd said that to her, because she did pitch in and try to be helpful. And there was a lot to learn. But he *was* starting to think of her as a princess. He was no prince, not even a knight, but he would save her from her dilemma if he could. It was obvious that she missed her family dreadfully, and he understood that the Christmas season was bringing that emotion into sharper focus for her.

"And I brought up a bottle of blackberry wine," he added.

"Mmm," Auburn said. "This is a feast."

That was all the praise he needed. Dillinger carved the

turkey, placed a slice on her plate, along with some potatoes and vegetables. He loaded his up, as well, and glanced at Rose sleeping peacefully in her cradle. "None for you, I'm afraid," he told the baby, and Auburn smiled.

"It's even too soon for us to mash some of this up and feed it to her," she said. "But by next year, she'll be ready for her own little plate of Christmas dinner."

Auburn wouldn't be here to see it, if he had anything to do about it. Dillinger watched her eat, enjoying her expression as she savored every mouthful. "Does it taste like turkey in your time?"

"It tastes fresher," she admitted. "Most of the time our food is frozen, though Mom buys her turkey at the butcher's market every year, fresh from a farm. Still, this somehow tastes even better."

"After dinner, I'm going to show you the moon and the stars," Dillinger told her. "Out here the sky is so black at night you can see stars for miles. We can stand on the porch and look at the full moon."

"I'd enjoy that."

They ate in silence for a while until Auburn finally said, "I'm stuffed."

He was, too. He hadn't been able to take his eyes off her the entire time, he realized, and hadn't paid attention to a single bite he put in his mouth. He was full of food but empty of love, a well inside him that was beginning to fill with Auburn. "Would you be more comfortable in one of Polly's dresses?" he asked slowly. "She was about your size…and you must be tired of wearing my clothes and those things you have on."

Auburn glanced down at the soft pants she called sweats. "I'm all right."

"You'd be warmer in a long dress and boots. I should have thought of it sooner." He felt stupid for not recalling that Polly had a closetful of clothes he hadn't been able to part with. "It would make me happy to know that her things were being put to use. For that matter, it would make Polly happy to know that her clothes aren't just sitting in a closet for no one to enjoy."

Auburn's gaze met his. "If you really think—"

"I do." He nodded. "I'll clean the table and you go back to Polly's closet and find something you'd like to wear." He felt good about this. A year was long enough to selfishly hold all of her memories to himself, especially when Auburn needed clothes so badly and wouldn't go to town to get any.

"Then I will. Thank you."

She got up from the table and went down the hall. He busied himself with storing the leftover turkey and washing the dishes. After about ten minutes had passed, he heard a small sound behind him.

Dillinger turned to find Auburn in a bottle-green worsted wool dress with long sleeves and a bell-shaped skirt. He smiled. "That's better."

"It fits perfectly, as if it was made for me. Thank you," Auburn said. "I actually was quite tired of my sweats."

He put the last of the dishes in the cupboard. "Let's go outside." She'd probably needed a break, and Rose was soundly sleeping for the moment so it was now or never.

On the wide porch, he pointed up to the sky. "Stars as far as the eye can see."

"Yes," Auburn said, her voice reverent, "it's lovely. We don't see this many stars in the city."

"Why?" He loved looking at the night sky, didn't think he could stand it if he couldn't see lots of stars.

"City lights, tall buildings, glare from neon signs." Auburn craned her neck to see the moon. "This is like a slice of heaven."

He'd always thought so. "I'm sorry I brought you here, into 1892."

She looked at him. "You believe me?"

"Yes, although I can't figure it out."

"I can't, either. But it happened."

"One thing I don't understand is that you said I levitated."

"You did. Twice."

"Why haven't you done that here? Shouldn't it work in reverse?"

"I don't know," she said. "It was really weird. And I saw your life when I held Polly's earring."

"I still can't believe simple gold earrings can be a charm. I'd rather believe in the kissing."

She laughed. "You don't want to kiss me."

"Yeah," he said, "I do."

Her eyes widened with surprise, the flood of starlight clearly illuminating her expression. "You do?"

"If it sends you back, sure, I'd kiss you."

"Right now?"

"This very instant."

He could feel her breath catch as she waited expectantly. "I'll hate to say goodbye to you," he said quietly, "but here goes nothing."

And then he pulled her into his arms and drew her lips to his, closing his eyes as he waited for the magic to steal her away from him.

A rifle shot rang out, echoing loudly in the clearing between the house and the forest. Shocked, Dillinger and Auburn jumped away from each other.

"Turkey hunter?" she asked with a gasp.

"Get in the house," Dillinger commanded.

THE BABY WAS STILL ASLEEP, even though Auburn's heart was beating loudly enough to wake the dead. The kiss hadn't worked! She was still here, and someone had taken a potshot at Dillinger. That gunfire hadn't sounded anything like the Old West show at Six Flags; it sounded much more serious than the rat-a-tat of fake shooting.

She was frightened. For him, and for herself. And Rose.

He came inside a few moments later, heading straight to the fireplace to warm up.

"Did you catch whoever it was?" Auburn asked.

"No."

"Was it an accident?"

"Don't think so."

She swallowed. "That doesn't make me feel better."

He turned to face her. "I'm sorry."

"Why would someone shoot at you?" Of course she knew the answer: he was a man who hunted people down and killed them. Eventually someone would want revenge.

He came over to her, taking a strand of her hair in one hand and smoothing it through his fingers. He touched her face gently. "I liked kissing you," he said, "and I have to say I'm glad you're still here with me."

Auburn felt herself begin to shake despite the warmth of his hands. "Why would someone shoot at you?" she asked again. "Do you know who it was?"

"I think I do," Dillinger said, "and I don't think they were shooting at me. I think they were shooting at you."

She felt space and time float around her, wondered if she was finally going to levitate. "I'm going to faint," she said, and the last thought she had was how glad she was that Dillinger was there to catch her.

WHEN AUBURN AWAKENED, she wasn't in her own bed. She knew instantly that she was in Dillinger's. How long she'd slept she wasn't certain, but not long enough to forget what had happened.

Dillinger must be wrong. No one wanted to shoot her; no one here knew her. "Dillinger," she whispered, feeling the other side of the bed for him.

Her hand connected with a solid, well-muscled back. "Huh?" he grunted.

"Are you awake?"

"I am now." He rolled over to face her. "Go back to sleep. I think you had too much blackberry wine."

"I think I didn't have enough. My plans are to have some for breakfast."

He grunted again, reached out a strong arm to pull her toward him and nestle her against him. "You talk too much and I have to get up at four to milk the cows. Go back to sleep."

She couldn't sleep! "Dillinger, no one here knows me. No one would want to kill me."

He rested his jaw on top of her head. "I'm going to put weight on your skull like this so your mouth will shut."

She wriggled from underneath his jaw. "You're just trying to scare me so I'll sleep with you."

"Never needed an excuse for a woman to sleep with me," Dillinger said with a head-splitting yawn. "Go to sleep, little one."

"Don't talk to me like a child!"

"You're acting like one."

She turned over to put herself nose-to-nose with her opinionated bedmate. "You accuse me of acting like a child when you won't even acknowledge that your career has come back to bite you in the butt."

"It was Polly's brother," he said.

She blinked, taking that in. "How do you know?"

"I found his tracks in the snow, know his shoe size and brand. Know the type of tobacco he smokes and could smell it in the air." His hands flexed at her waist, rolling her back over again, repositioning her the way he wanted her.

"So go to his house and ask him what the heck he wants," Auburn said, "because it's not me."

"I don't want him to know that I know," Dillinger said. "It's likely he would consider it his duty to kill any woman who tried to replace his sister."

Auburn sat up, punched a finger against a remarkably firm chest. "And you were going to tell me this when?"

"Never. I thought Pierre was in Alaska. Didn't cross my mind that a year trapping hadn't worn away his anger at me for letting his sister die."

"Letting her die? You didn't want Polly to die."

"I know. But he thinks I didn't do enough to help her. Actually, he thinks she got pneumonia because she was trying to run away from me, and as you may have noted, it's quite a distance in the snow from here just to the forest, much less to town."

"She was far too independent for that," Auburn said. "Even I know she would have just hitched up your buggy or your sleigh and hotfooted it out of here if she'd wanted to badly enough."

"Buggies won't move in this snow."

"So you're saying she tried to walk? She was too intelligent for that." Auburn had spent a lot of time going through Polly's belongings. The woman had been a lot of things, but dumb as a rock was not one of them. She'd been a talented seamstress; her cupboards were neat, and the few drawings and paintings sprinkled throughout the house were well done. Polly had been a woman able to make creative use of her time on a ranch so remote that most people would go crazy from the lack of human companionship.

"She hitched the sleigh. It didn't make it. She was caught between here and town. She was in the snow for a very long time before I found her by following the sleigh tracks. She wasn't an experienced driver."

Auburn heard the quiet edge in his voice. "So she was going to town."

"Yes, but…she was going to see about a baby who'd just been born and was very ill. Polly loved children, desperately wanted a baby of our own. She knew the mother needed help, and went to see if she could bring the baby here while the woman recovered from her birthing fever."

Auburn turned toward Dillinger. "I'm so sorry," she said softly against his cheek, and this time when he took her in his arms, she hoped he planned on doing more than kissing her. She needed to feel his heartbeat against hers, wanted to give him the comfort he so much needed.

But he pulled back from her. "This is a bad idea," he whispered, though he placed a gentle kiss against her lips. "I knew sleeping in the same bed with you would lead to temptations no mortal man could resist. I'm no prince, you know."

"Dillinger, come to me," she whispered.

"I have no way of keeping you from conceiving a child. And what if you are sent back to your own place and time? If you were pregnant with my baby, it would be very difficult for you. I couldn't stand wondering whether I had a child in the future that couldn't name me as his father."

"Oh," Auburn said, glad that was all that was bothering him, "I won't become pregnant." She kissed the tip of his nose, trying to tempt him to her. But he was so stubborn, she realized. More stubborn than she was.

"How do you know?" he demanded.

"One of the many wonders of my century is a small

device a woman wears all the time that keeps her from getting pregnant."

His hands roamed under her bottom, bunching her dress up. "How?"

"By blocking things." She cleared her throat. "That's all the explanation you need of women and the sexual revolution."

"Between that and the plastic diaper, I'm beginning to think I should have stayed in your time with you." Dillinger reached around to begin unbuttoning the back of her dress. "And this works every time?"

He sounded as if he thought she was telling a fairy tale he greatly wanted to believe, and yet was afraid the book would be ripped away from him before the happy ending. She put her hand over him, finding exactly what she wanted. "Yes," she said, and then whispered against his lips, "Dillinger, show me the stars."

He hesitated for just an instant, grappling with a hundred questions and a thousand demons, but Auburn was too sweet, too soft and much too willing for him to resist. He allowed himself to melt into her, and again wondered if this woman had been brought through space and time to be with him.

He so badly wanted to believe.

Chapter Twelve

Auburn awakened to an empty bed, though she wasn't surprised, since the cows came first. "Darn Bessie anyway," she said, sitting up. "Although she does make a good breakfast for you every morning…" She peeked over the side of the bed to find Rose.

The baby wasn't in her cradle. Auburn jumped out of bed and into the green dress, hurrying to go help Dillinger. She found him in the kitchen, holding the child and making pancakes.

"What are you doing?" Auburn demanded, feeling self-conscious, since she hadn't brushed her hair in her haste to take over baby care. Wasn't that her job? Caring for the baby and sometimes cooking when she could get the food preparation figured out? She reached to take Rose from him.

"Making flapjacks," Dillinger said, not looking at

her. "Little Miss Sunshine wanted out of her cradle at the break of dawn."

"Why didn't you wake me?" Auburn asked. "I could have gotten up to help."

"You were snoring," he said. "I thought you were probably tired."

Dillinger had kept her up for many delightful hours, certainly, and yes, she'd appreciated the recuperative sleep, but did she sense a slight reserve on his part?

"Hey," she said, moving next to him, where he couldn't avoid eye contact, "I don't mind doing my job."

"I can take care of a baby through some winter months," Dillinger replied, managing to avoid looking at her as he slid some pancakes onto a plate. "You don't have to stay because of us."

The obvious answer was *I'd go if I knew how,* but Auburn decided maybe this cowboy, like many other men, did his best communicating after his stomach was full. So she let his remark pass, and laid the plates on the table. "This smells heavenly."

He sat down and began to eat. It was unlike him not to be chivalrous and wait on her, but maybe he was a cranky guy on occasion. Auburn set the baby in her lap and started on her own pancakes.

After a moment, she realized he was staring at her. "What?" she asked. "Is something wrong?"

He looked at her for a long time. Prickles ran over her skin as he studied her. "Dillinger?"

"Eat," he said at last, and resumed demolishing his food.

Something was wrong. He definitely had a bug up his hiney about something, but Auburn couldn't mind-read, so she shrugged and decided to let him work his kinks out on his own.

FOR LUNCH, AUBURN decided to make turkey soup. They had plenty of the huge bird left, and surely she couldn't mess up a basic broth and veggies. She lugged a cast-iron pot to the stove during Rose's naptime, then carted some water from the well to start her stock. A few moments were wasted as she considered what to substitute for bullion or boxed broth, then she tossed some butter and a chopped onion into a skillet and sautéed that with some of the blackberry wine she snitched from Dillinger's hiding place. He probably wouldn't appreciate thinking she was "tippling" at eleven in the morning, so she was careful and quick about her pilfering. Carrots, potatoes, some cabbage and even a few dried mushrooms followed the turkey into the pot. Salt and pepper finished off her recipe and she set it to simmer.

She dusted every inch of the house, trying to keep herself occupied. Sweeping the floors didn't take long, and after an hour of Dillinger's absence, she finally heard the sound of stamping boots on the porch. At last he was back! "I hope you're over your silent treatment," she called out, flinging open the door.

The man on the porch was definitely not Dillinger, and he didn't look all that friendly, either. A slow smile came over his lips under a handlebar mustache, but it wasn't a nice smile. He looked more as if he was baring his teeth, especially as he took in her green dress, and Auburn wished she had her frying pan so she could give him a good roundhouse smack. "Yes?" she asked, her tone cool as the outdoors.

"Are you the lady of the house?" he asked.

She stiffened. "Absolutely *not*."

That seemed to take him aback. "You're not?"

"No. If you want to speak to the owner, he should be back anytime." Auburn tried to close the door, but he held it open with a boot.

"Tell Dillinger that Pierre called on him," he said. "And a word of warning—he'll try to kill you, just like he killed my sister. A man who kills easily can't change."

"If Dillinger killed your sister, why isn't he in jail?" Auburn demanded.

"They're afraid. The sheriff's a dolt. No one wants to mess with a man with a reputation for cold-blooded murder. But I am not afraid of him. You should be."

Auburn slammed the door, quickly locking it. She

rubbed her arms to stave off the chills running over her. "Eww," she said, "Dillinger is not going to be happy."

He came in the back door a half hour later, a load of firewood in his arms. By then Auburn had her hair brushed and put in a ponytail, and had fortified herself with the thought that her soup was coming along nicely.

"Pierre came by to see you," she said airily, and Dillinger dropped the logs next to the fireplace with a thud.

"Pierre?" His eyes narrowed.

"That's what he said." She nodded. "As in South Dakota."

"Did you open the door?"

"Yes, I did."

"Don't ever do that again."

"Well, excuse me, but you never said I shouldn't before. And anyway, I thought it was you coming home."

He sniffed the air. "What's that smell?"

"Soup."

"Soup?" He seemed stunned.

"As in turkey, broth and veggies? Maybe some rice or barley if you've got it on hand? A side of bread, if you're lucky? That kind of soup."

He studied her, his gaze going from her head to her feet, where the Uggs poked out beneath her hem. "Auburn, about last night..."

"Oh, *now* you want to talk!" she exclaimed. He couldn't call all the shots on moods. "Listen, cowboy, first you need to clarify the rules with me. I didn't know anything about not opening doors, and your pronouncement seems kind of bossy to me, especially because it's pretty lonely out here. I might even get really joyful about having a Fuller Brush salesperson drop by."

"When someone shoots at you from the forest, you can probably assume you don't want to go outside or make yourself a target. I shouldn't have to tell you that."

She blinked. "Dillinger, I'm from New York City. We go out. That's what we do. There are thousands of people walking around all the time, the lights are always on, it never feels unsafe. It would never have occurred to me to confine myself to the house, when there are chores needing to be done, like emptying the infernal chamber pot and getting water from the well. Besides," she said, highly annoyed, "I really think he was aiming at you. If Pierre was the shooter, he had plenty of time to do me in today, since you were off hiding your emotions somewhere."

He grimaced. "I was not hiding my emotions."

"What else would you call it?" She put her hands on her hips in the starchiest manner she could muster. "We spend a wonderful night together, and in the morning, you don't even bother to say, 'So I hope you saw those stars you were all hot to see.'" She had seen stars, lots of them, and she'd been dying to tell him how wonderful it had been in his big, strong arms.

The sinfully sexy lout.

"I thought you'd be gone," he said. "I was hoping you would be."

She stared at him. "As in taking a long walk?"

"As in back to your century."

She was just a little hurt. "Oh, I get it. When the kiss didn't send me magically out of your life, you gave yourself permission to go for the extra push, a little boost to the recipe. If a kiss wasn't the talisman, then making love had to kick-start the spell. And surely you couldn't feel unfaithful to Polly's memory if you were just helping a poor lost woman get home."

Auburn could tell he was not happy with her right now.

"Well, maybe we need a second try," she said brightly. "The second time's probably the charm."

He didn't think that was funny. If anything, his eyes grew darker. "I'm sorry it didn't work out the way you wanted it to."

He turned back to stoke the fire. Auburn ignored a bit of heartbreak in her soul, and went to stir the soup after she checked on Rose, who was just beginning to wake up, probably in response to their unhappy tones. *Great. This is sort of like being single in the twenty-first century, with the whole Men Are From Mars thing.*

And on top of that, she had Polly's brother running around with his issues.

Blast.

This was not the recuperative drive-across-America-and-experience-the-rest-of-the-continent jaunt she'd had in mind when she'd hit the road to clear her head after ditching her fiancé.

On the other hand, it wasn't as bad as being married to Bradley would have been. Auburn sneaked a look at Dillinger, who was staring out the window, searching the landscape, probably hunting for his boob of a brother-in-law.

Okay, Polly, girlfriend, she thought, *if you brought me here to make a family with these two, if this is your idea of a heavenly rescue, Mr. Stubborn's probably going to require a bit of a kick in the pants.*

And feel free to make it just a slightly harder kick than necessary, if you want.

MAYBE HE WAS GOING snow mad. Winter crazy. Becoming light-deprived. The woman and her tales were beginning to alter him. Or he was changing when he really didn't think he should. He hadn't expected such fullness of spirit when he'd held her in his arms last night. Auburn had surprised him. She was welcoming and responsive, doing the duty a wife normally did, and seemed to very much enjoy sharing pleasure with him.

Polly had been sweet like that, too, which he missed more than anything.

In fact, he'd felt unfaithful and conflicted afterward,

and though he knew it didn't make sense, he really had hoped Auburn would get snatched away by some heavenly hand, to the place where she belonged, wherever that was.

At the breakfast table, when she'd sat there so prettily with Rose in her arms, wearing Polly's dress, he'd nearly choked on his guilt. It was what he and Polly had so hoped for, Polly making pilgrimages to church in town dutifully every Sunday to pray for a baby.

He had failed her in that. What man couldn't get his wife with child?

Now he had a family of sorts, and he didn't know if he deserved them. Or wanted them. Or where they'd come from.

He stared out the window, seeing the track of boot prints left in the snow. Pierre didn't care that Dillinger knew he was out there, and neither did Dillinger. If he wanted, he could step outside right now and find him, kill him if he wished. He was the gunslinger, Pierre a trapper. It wouldn't be much of a fight.

But Dillinger had no urge to fight. He'd given up his livelihood for Polly, and taken up ranching and farming. He would not dishonor her memory by returning to it, and certainly not by killing her brother.

Though he would destroy Pierre if he ever laid a finger on Auburn.

What Dillinger was going to do about the story-spinning woman he wasn't certain. He couldn't just sleep with her every night, as if she were his wife; that would be wrong, most especially to her. She deserved better than what he had to offer.

He wanted to take her into his bedroom right now and apologize for all the rough things he'd said, kiss away the hurt he knew he'd caused her. Those doe eyes could soften with tender feelings to the point that it made him want to hold her, tell her she was an angel brought to bear light on his misery. What would be left for him if she and Rose disappeared? Surely they could not stay; they were not his to begin with.

The long, cruel claws of winter would once again crush his spirit.

"Dillinger?" Auburn said softly. "Do you want a bowl of Christmas turkey soup?"

He didn't turn from the window, but closed his eyes against the winter landscape outside, and his ears against the sound of her sweet voice.

He didn't want the soup, damn it.

He wanted *her*.

Chapter Thirteen

The next day, Auburn reached out with nervous fingers to touch the hidden journal she'd found in the writing desk. She'd discovered a secret drawer quite by accident after whacking her head as she straightened up from a crouched position, while sweeping up some dust. "Darn dust bunnies," she'd muttered, wishing she could conk Dillinger on the head so *he'd* see stars. And a drawer had popped open like magic.

There lay a green journal, leather-bound with gold letters. Auburn didn't need to open it to know it was Polly's treasured private thoughts. She gave the journal a stroke with her fingertips before hastily closing the drawer. Atop the desk, Polly's small self-portrait smiled serenely, her single earring shining beside it.

The writing desk was a shrine in some ways, and Auburn never touched the items here. It was all Dillinger had of his wife, besides her clothes, and what good did those do him? Here were her favorite things.

Of course, Auburn itched to learn what Polly had written in the hours she spent alone, while Dillinger was out doing his work. "You know," she told the portrait, "girl talk should go two ways. Reading your journal wouldn't be right. If you want me to read it, you'll have to let me know."

Nothing happened. Auburn left the desk and moved into the kitchen with her broom. The snow that got tramped into the house brought tiny bits of dirt and torn leaves with it, no matter how careful they tried to be about wiping their feet. The nicely fitted wood floors needed a daily sweeping to keep clean.

When she'd gone from corporate vice president to housemaid and chimney watcher, she wasn't certain. Somehow it wasn't all that bad, but maybe it was like summer camp, and she'd get tired of it after a few weeks. Sessions at the exclusive Walden Lake Summer Camp for Girls had always seemed so exciting, but by the fifth week—her parents liked her gone all season so she could learn "proper manners that all the girls from the best families know"—Auburn was tired of the spiders and the heat and the dirt and pillow fights, fun as it always was in the beginning.

She wondered if maybe she was just one of those women who bored easily. Look how quickly she'd tired of Bradley in just two short years. Why hadn't she realized he wasn't the right man for her more quickly?

Why hadn't she looked over the corporate books more carefully and discovered there was a problem?

Maybe, she decided with a pang, she'd been too content to let other people do things for her.

Polly had been an independent woman. While she'd lived in a time that had necessitated a certain version of women's roles, Polly had not been dependent on her husband for her entertainment and identity. She'd been a helpmate, not helpless.

Auburn was learning a lot from her example.

She went back to the desk, slowly picked up the earring, admiring it. Wondered where the other one was and if they'd ever find it. Gave it a small shake to hear the bells tinkle—and screamed when Bradley came crashing into the room like a drunken sailor.

She tossed the earring to the desk. "Bradley!"

He shook his head, dazed. "What?"

"What are you doing here?"

He looked at her, clearly confused. "Auburn?"

Oh, God, this was a nightmare. "Go, go," she said, giving him a couple of light shoves with the broom. "Go home to your own century."

He stood, brushing himself off. His round glasses were slightly askew, his hair rumpled. "Jeez, what the hell just happened? Auburn, quit sweeping at me."

What rotten luck for him to find her, all the way back in 1892. She pressed herself against the writing desk, hoping he was an apparition that would suddenly disappear.

"Why are you wearing that ugly dress?" Bradley asked, "and whose brat is that?"

Gasping, she picked up Rose. "Don't you call this sweet baby a brat!"

"Whatever." He brushed a few wrinkles from his shirt and his designer jeans. "I'm not very happy with you right now."

"I don't think I was ever happy with you, but never mind that," Auburn said. "How did you get here?"

"I have no idea," he stated. "One minute I was sitting on the bed in your hotel room, and the next second I'm here." He grinned, his blond good looks not having any effect on her. "I knew I'd find you eventually."

"You found me. You can go back now. Click your heels together. Do something that will reverse whatever you did."

"Whatever's cooking smells awesome." He strolled into the kitchen. "Fancy setup you've got here. Who made the soup?"

"I did," she said between gritted teeth, and he laughed. "You don't cook."

Auburn sighed. "You need to go before Dillinger finds you here."

"Dillinger? Is that the guy you've been shacking up with?"

She frowned. "I'm not shacking up with anybody!"

"The security guard at your penthouse in Dallas told me you'd left with some cowboy and his kid. I'll give you kids, Auburn, if you're all hot to get pregnant. Your parents would love to be grandparents."

She hated his confident smirk. "It's over between us, Bradley, if I didn't make that perfectly clear."

"I don't think so. Your parents owe me a lot of money. In fact, they owe me the company." He gazed at her, trying to make his expression sympathetic and failing miserably.

"That will have to be their problem," she said softly, and Bradley's eyebrows rose.

"You don't care about McGinnis Perfumes?"

Slowly she shook her head. "Even if I knew how to get back home, I care about what I have here more."

"What? A baby? An unemployed roughneck?"

"Roughneck?"

"Redneck, whatever. Can't be much if he's got you stuck out on a farm in the middle of nowhere. You're a city girl, Auburn, a world traveler. You don't belong here."

He might be right, but she didn't need her life's big truths pointed out to her by a man who had ten pairs of golf shoes and eight expensive cars. "Don't worry about me. I'll be fine."

The front door burst open, kicked with force. Auburn

let out a yelp, and just to make her nightmare complete, Pierre walked in, looking like a wolf among lambs.

"What have we here?" he asked, "a weasel in the henhouse? What will Dillinger think?"

"Pierre," Auburn said, "get *out*. Both of you disappear." Clearly, her fairy godmother had gone on strike.

The men looked at her, then shook hands with each other, instantly realizing they were on the same team. Auburn rolled her eyes. "If you're both quite done, I have to take care of Rose. And we don't want you here, so please leave. I have a feeling everything will go downhill from here if you don't depart at once."

They looked at one another and shrugged.

"I'll stay for dinner," Pierre stated.

"I'm not going anywhere," Bradley added. "I don't know how I got here."

"If there's witchcraft going on here, that would be very interesting to the authorities in town," Pierre mused.

"There is no witchcraft, Pierre," Auburn said. "And if you don't hush that kind of talk, I'm going to pull a spell of whup-ass out of my cauldron and give you a lesson in social etiquette you sorely need." She sidled over to her frying pan, ready to inflict damage if either of them got any more weird on her.

Fortunately, Dillinger walked in at that moment.

"Why is the door open?" he demanded. "You're going to freeze to— What the hell is going on in here?"

He positively glowered at Bradley and Pierre, as if he'd like to kill them both with his stare.

"Boys club," Auburn said. "I can't convince them this house isn't a good meeting place."

"Get out," he commanded Pierre and Bradley, seeming to grow taller and meaner right before her eyes. His gaze narrowed and his hands went to his hips, then down his legs in a movement he must have made many times before. He'd been feeling for pistols out of habit, then remembered his promise to Polly.

Auburn shrank into the kitchen with the baby, eyeing her collection of pots and pans. If Dillinger went for one of their visitors, she could bean the other. A cast-iron skillet ought to leave a headache for a few days that would incapacitate any man.

"Auburn, take the baby and go into the back of the house," Dillinger told her.

"I'm…I'm staying," Auburn insisted, not about to leave him alone in a two-on-one fight. "I have to stir the soup."

She peeked at him from the doorway. He glared at her and she raised her chin.

Then he ignored her. "If either of you have something to say, get on with it and get out."

"Auburn is my fiancée, and she's coming back with me." Bradley seemed intimidated by Dillinger, but put on a brave face, probably because he felt he had a buddy in Pierre.

Pierre laughed. "This is too much fun."

"I don't think so," Auburn snapped. "I am *not* your fiancée, Bradley."

Dillinger looked at her. "This is the man you were going to marry?"

She nodded.

He raised one eyebrow, communicating his disdain.

"It seemed like a good idea at the time," Auburn said.

"Hey!"

"Oh, hush," she muttered. "You don't want me, Bradley. You're just trying to get the company away from my parents and me. You've done it. Congratulate yourself, accept that I'm not coming back with you, and take yourself home to New York."

They all stared at each other for a moment, then Auburn walked back into the main room and held out her hand to Bradley. "Give me the earring."

"What earring?" He seemed confused.

"You must have an earring somewhere on you," she said, knowing he had to have Polly's other earring or he wouldn't be here. A lot of things were beginning to make sense to her. The earrings, the baby, seeing Polly…this all had to do with Dillinger's wife.

But Auburn didn't want Bradley to know about the earrings or he'd take the set, use them to trip around the world in every century and somehow manage to profit from it.

"Oh, yeah. Is this yours?" he asked, handing her back the tiny belled bauble. "It didn't look like something you'd wear. You've always been a pearls kind of girl."

"True," Auburn said, "but change is good." She grabbed the earring, sneaked its mate from the writing desk and went to hide them in Dillinger's bedroom. They were his wife's earrings, his gift to her, and if they had a magical property of some kind, it was up to him to decide what to do with them.

She hoped he'd let her use them to get back home, but that was a conversation for another day. Going back into the main room, she saw Dillinger, Pierre and Bradley locked in a fierce glaring contest.

"Oh, for heaven's sake," she said, "the snow is coming down in clumps. You two had better head off, because I'm sure Dillinger doesn't want you to stay here."

Bradley looked around the well-built farmhouse. "I don't know. This is a pretty cool place. I've always wanted a house like this, far away from the city."

Auburn stared at him. "No, you haven't."

He nodded. "Yes, I did. Just too busy trying to keep up with your jet-set lifestyle to think of my own needs."

She raised her brows. "That's news to me."

"It would be," Bradley said piteously. "You never realized I had any."

"Any…what?" Auburn asked, curious in spite of herself.

"Needs."

"Oh, jeez." She looked at Dillinger. "Are you hungry? Are you ready for some soup? If you get rid of these two, I can have your dinner on the table in a jiff."

Bradley gazed at her with admiration. "I like this new housewifely you."

A small light came into Dillinger's eyes. "I was afraid you might have second thoughts, now that you see him again."

She did have second thoughts, but they were the same ones she'd had when Bradley had flown into the room: *How do I get rid of him once and for all?* "There is no interplanetary trash can big enough to hold him," she said.

"Hey!" Bradley yelped again.

"Pierre, you and I will have to settle our score another day," Dillinger said. "There are too many eyewitnesses for you to kill me now."

Auburn sucked in a breath. She looked at Pierre, whose dark-eyed gaze had been following everything with interest.

"I don't need to kill you today," Pierre said, "it's too much fun watching you squirm. We'll stay here tonight, me and my new friend, Bradley." He grinned, and Auburn thought it was a shame he was a weasel because he wasn't totally unattractive—he had a lot of Polly's good facial features.

"There's no room in the inn," Auburn said, "is there,

Dillinger?" If these two stayed, she wouldn't be able to cast her lures his way, and she'd discovered the wonders of keeping warm in bed with a certain strong, sexy cowboy. Selfishly, she wanted Bradley and Pierre gone sooner rather than later.

"We'll sleep in this room," Pierre said. "The fur blanket will be the best bed I've had in a long time."

"I can handle that," Bradley agreed. "I want to take a look over this spread you've got, Dillinger. These are great digs."

Dillinger didn't look flattered. "Didn't you get here by sleigh, Pierre? You can leave the same way."

"No," he replied cheerfully. "Sleigh runner's broken, and you wouldn't turn a traveler out to freeze, would you?" He took off his Western hat and jacket, tossing them on the divan. "*Farmer's Almanac* says this may be the coldest, longest winter on record."

"Lovely," Auburn said wryly. "Dillinger?"

"I'll sleep in here with them," he sighed. "I can't turn Polly's brother out into a blinding snowstorm. Nor this city-slicker, either." He shot Bradley a disdainful glare. "Put the soup on, please, Auburn."

"But they want to kill you!" she argued.

"I don't," Bradley said.

"There's time for that later," Pierre added.

Auburn ignored them both. "Why do you have to sleep out here with them?" she asked Dillinger. "I mean,

Rose and I always sleep in the guest room," she said hurriedly, not wanting to get a bunch of negative feedback on that topic, "but you should at least sleep in your own bed."

She was terrified that Pierre would try something as soon as Dillinger nodded off. If she had her way, Dillinger would be locked up tight in his bedroom and Pierre and Bradley would sleep in a barn far away from the house. Actually, they only deserved the outhouse, but Dillinger was in the mood to be hospitable.

"I have to keep any eye on them, Auburn," Dillinger said. "It's best to keep your enemies close to your bosom. Biblically speaking."

Great. She wished he hadn't said "bosom." It made her think about what wonderful things he'd done to hers, but it appeared they would be staying under wraps tonight. She went to put soup in bowls, slice some bread and pour wine.

Auburn wondered what she could do to send Bradley back home as soon as possible. She was itching to ask Polly. She had a funny feeling the woman in the picture frame knew.

Chapter Fourteen

The sight of the three men sprawled in the parlor in a triangular standoff—recline-off, as they all had with their backs propped against furniture, rifles across their laps, their western hats pulled low over their faces—was more than Auburn could bear. "This is the room I'm going to put the Christmas tree in," she said, "and you three are definitely not cheery seasonal ornaments. Could we at least put the firearms away?"

She held Rose tightly, afraid to step any farther into the room. One might have thought that after a delicious, if she did say so herself, meal of soup and wine, the testosterone levels would have gone down a bit. Who wouldn't feel relaxed in front of a cozy fire? It wasn't as if there was central heating in the house, so as far as she was concerned, the three of them were in the lap of luxury, while she was making do with a warming pan.

And no Dillinger to snuggle with for warmth and maybe a little sizzle.

"We're fine, Auburn," Dillinger said. "Go back to bed."

"How can anyone sleep, knowing that the three of you are prepared to blow each other's heads off?" Auburn was certain nothing good could come of three men sleeping with their toys, the big babies. "It would work just as well, I'm sure, if all of you held Bibles or something," she said sweetly, and was rewarded by two very black glares.

Bradley didn't look quite as annoyed; his expression might have even been a tad relieved, because he seemed somewhat perturbed by the whole gun show, though he was clearly going for bravado in front of the other two men. She didn't think he'd ever even held a gun before.

"Bradley, put that weapon away," she said. "You look totally silly."

"They gave me the smallest one," Bradley muttered sheepishly. "Dillinger said I might need it in case a bear tries to get in."

She looked at Dillinger. "A bear?"

He shrugged.

"Oh, for pity's sake. I'm going to bed. You three are all going to help drag in a tree tomorrow for me to decorate, and you're going to mind your manners and not track in mud or anything, or I'm not cooking any turkey pie tomorrow." She sniffed. "I'm going to make it with potatoes and not noodles, but I'm pretty sure I can make a very good whipping cream to put in it if I'm not upset by too much male dominance in my house."

Oops. Major tactical blunder.

Dillinger looked pleased with her use of the possessive pronoun, Bradley looked unhappy and Pierre looked amused. "My house because I'm staying here for now, with this baby, the only person here who seems to have any sense," Auburn said. "Good night, Three Stooges."

And then she went to put Rose in her cradle and herself in bed—not very happy about being robbed of a night in Dillinger's arms.

What if last night had been the last time she'd ever get to hold him?

She hoped Bradley hadn't used up the magic window or whatever it was that had allowed her and Dillinger to time travel. Otherwise, they might be stuck here. All of them, including Dillinger's vengeful brother-in-law.

She had a bad feeling that Pierre was just biding his time before he made his move.

AUBURN AWAKENED INSTANTLY when someone got in bed with her. "If that's you, Bradley, you're about to lose your family jewels!" she hissed.

Dillinger's chuckle warmed her. "It's me, my gentle little pussycat."

"Whatever," Auburn said, instantly going into his

arms. "What if I said, 'Gee, Bradley, what took you so long to get here?'"

He growled against her hair, holding her tightly to him. "I'd spank you."

"So did you cart their carcasses off to the forest?" Auburn murmured against Dillinger's chin.

"A bloodthirsty woman," Dillinger said, tweaking her bottom. "I'm getting to know you better all the time."

"So did you?" Dillinger wouldn't be here if he hadn't tied them up or buried them under twelve feet of snow.

"Just put a little medicine in their wine at the table." He tweaked her nipple gently, drawing a surprised, pleased gasp from her. "You didn't think I was going to let them spoil my time alone with you?"

"I should hope not," she said, doing a little tweaking of her own and drawing the desired response from the eager male in her bed. "Though I did wonder."

He nibbled at her lower lip, and she nestled closer in his arms, as near to his heartbeat as she could get.

"You should have faith, little one."

"I'd feel so much better if they weren't here," she said.

"Shh," Dillinger whispered as he held her tightly, easing her fears. And so Auburn held on to him and enjoyed the pleasure she found in his arms.

By the time Rose let out a little squeak iin the morning, Auburn was alone again in the bed, but it didn't matter. She knew Dillinger wasn't worried about Bradley being here. In fact, he wasn't worried about much of anything, except making her happy.

And that was enough to make her start thinking about whether she could stay with Dillinger forever.

But she must have unfinished business with Bradley, as Dillinger and Pierre did with one another, and this was time's way of smoothing everything out for their eventual happiness.

She got up, made herself presentable, fed Rose, sang a quick morning lullaby to her and went to see what the men were up to.

The two males were lounging in the living room. "Where's Dillinger?" she asked them.

"Gone to look at his livestock," Pierre said.

She raised a brow. "You didn't go with him?"

"Would you have trusted me to?" he asked with a toothy grin.

"More than I'd trust you here," Auburn retorted.

Bradley looked at her. "I'd protect you, Auburn."

"With that popgun?" she asked, glancing at the pistol Bradley had stuck in a holster he'd found. "What makes you think I trust you more than Pierre, anyway?"

"Auburn!" Bradley exclaimed. "How can you say that about a man you were going to marry?"

"Not trusting each other isn't good," Pierre said, laughing. "You're probably better off without each other."

Auburn sighed and went into the kitchen. Maybe

she'd whip up some eggs and bacon. She'd seen bacon in the larder and Dillinger brought in eggs from the chickens each day. She wondered how the gunslinger liked his eggs cooked, and decided he'd be so cold when he came in he wouldn't care if they were fried or scrambled as long as they were hot.

"Auburn, can I talk to you?" Bradley murmured, coming into the kitchen.

"If you must," she replied, looking at the frying pans and trying to decide which would be best for the amount of eggs she was going to end up serving three hungry men.

"Your mother and father miss you," Bradley said.

She turned to stare at him. "Are you insane?"

"What?" His expression was one of total innocence.

"You're the reason I'm not with my parents right now."

"Nonsense. We just had a misunderstanding," Bradley said. "You're such a sensitive girl."

"You gave my parents a loan with terms they couldn't possibly meet in this economy, and you say I'm sensitive? How about just plain intelligent?" She chose a frying pan and went on with her preparations. "Scoot, Bradley. I can't think with you under my feet, and I'm trying to get the hang of this stove."

"I think you gave up on us too hastily."

"No," Auburn said, "I gave up on us not a moment too soon, and several moments too late."

"That is so cold!"

"Bradley, what are you really doing here? I wish you'd go back and get your life in order. There's no reason for your presence."

"I can't go back. I don't even know how I got here."

She had a feeling she did, but she darn well wasn't going to give him Polly's earrings so he could take off and leave her stuck in the past.

"All I can figure is that you wanted to see me, Auburn. There's no other explanation for it. I think you're telling me one thing, but your heart says another. I believe we're meant to be together."

She handed Rose to Bradley. "Can you at least hold her so I can make some breakfast?"

"I— Okay." He took the baby as if she were a time bomb.

"First of all," Auburn said, cracking eggs into a bowl, "we are not meant to be together."

"You're not staying here, are you?" Bradley asked, his tone horrified. "Your parents wouldn't like that."

"I'll let you know after I've figured it out myself. I don't really know how I got here, either, so going back isn't exactly like buying a ticket to Paris. Now a little butter," she murmured, sliding some into the pan she was heating.

"It's so weird watching you be Mrs. Cleaver," Bradley said with a smile. "I would have proposed sooner if I'd known you were going to be Suzy Homemaker."

"Say one more thing like that and you'll find an egg cracked over your head," she said, her nerves already wearing thin with his commentary. Why hadn't she ever noticed how boring Bradley was?

Because I was busy doing what my parents wanted, which was being a good heiress, making a good match and settling down for the good of the McGinnis family name.

She'd lost a lot of time trying to be a good girl and socialite, climbing the right social ladders. On the other hand, she was certainly making up for it now. She smiled, thinking about how thoroughly Dillinger had loved her last night.

She doubted her parents would approve of her getting it on with a gunslinger, but hey, this was 1892, right?

"Bradley, take Rose out and put her in her cradle, will you, please?" Auburn asked, and just then Dillinger blew through the front door, carried on a snowy wind, dragging a wonderful fir tree behind him.

She smiled. "Hey, Superman."

Dillinger looked at her, confused. "Who?"

"Did you cut that all by yourself?" she asked, going to admire his handiwork.

"And dragged it half a mile, too." He was sweaty, but pleased that she liked his surprise.

"With drifts that high?"

"Snowshoes," he said. "There's too much snow even for horses today."

She flicked a stray wood chip off his flannel shirt and said, "You're probably starving after all that muscleman work. I have eggs in the kitchen for you."

Dillinger grinned, and it was like they were the only two people in the room, the only two people in the whole galaxy.

Bradley sighed. "I'll serve myself."

"She forgot the bacon, but I can fry that," Pierre said.

Auburn smiled at Dillinger. "What would you have done if you'd come home and I'd dinged both of them with a frying pan?"

He laughed, then gave her a long kiss he didn't seem to care about anybody seeing. "I would have thanked you."

Auburn was so happy she felt as if she were floating.

And then she realized she was.

Chapter Fifteen

Auburn floated only for a moment, and maybe just a couple of inches off the ground. She wasn't sure if anyone had noticed, but then Pierre said, "Witchcraft! That's it. I'm ready to kill both of you." He raised his rifle.

Bradley looked alarmed.

"I came here to kill you. I've only waited because there are two eyewitnesses and the snow is so deep it'll take me forever to walk back, unless my sleigh magically repairs itself."

"It didn't," Dillinger told him. "I hacked it into bits before I chopped down this tree." He shook the fir a little to make certain no more snow was caught in the branches, then propped it against a wall.

"You chopped up my sleigh?" Pierre lost his icy composure for the first time. "That's it, gunslinger. You're first. Get away from the woman so I don't splatter her with your blood." He aimed the rifle at Dillinger, suddenly coughing as he did so.

Auburn gasped. "Have you gone mad? What exactly is your problem?"

"The problem," Pierre said, his coughing fit racking him, his eyes glazing a bit, "is that you're wearing my sister's clothes, you're in my sister's house, and you're making *him* forget she ever existed."

"I don't think so," Auburn snapped. "The house is practically a shrine to your sister. Even I enjoy her being around." She frowned. "I don't get the sense that she was as mercenary as you."

Pierre couldn't seem to stop coughing, so he waved a hand and shook his head in lieu of arguing.

"Are you sick?" Bradley demanded. "Because if you are, I don't think you should be in the same room with the baby, or the food or us, for that matter."

Bradley had always been a bit of a germaphobe. Auburn stepped in front of Dillinger, prepared to shield him with her body. "Look, Pierre, your sister wouldn't mind me borrowing her clothes. She'd lend them to me herself if she were alive. She'd say it was practical, and probably would have given her clothes to anyone who needed them. And frankly, I think she'd be a bit embarrassed by the way you're behaving. It doesn't speak well for the family name."

He scowled at her. "You're in love with a gunslinger. What's that going to do for *your* family name?"

"Ouch," Bradley said. "She's not in love with him. She's going to marry me."

"Right," Pierre drawled. "That'll happen when this hellhole thaws out."

"Hey!" Bradley glanced around the room. "I happen to think this is a sweet setup. I wouldn't mind living here myself."

"I don't know why," Pierre said. "It's the middle of nowhere. And it's colder out here than in town. I think all the damn trees block the sun."

He bent over, coughing, and Auburn said, "You *are* sick!"

She went to touch his forehead, not that she wanted to. But she didn't want him filling Rose's living space with germs. "You have a high fever, Pierre," she said. "You'll just have to do your vengeful act another day. Go get in bed in the guest room. And I'm not cleaning out your chamber pot, so don't make a mess. I expect that room to be daisy-fresh when you move out."

He shook his head, coughed harder. "No."

"Yes," she said, firmly steering him toward the back room. "Trust me, we don't want you here, but you can barely hold that gun straight, so you can't shoot Dillinger today. I'd send for the sheriff and make him drag you off to get well in a jail cell, but Dillinger says no one can get out of here."

"That's what happened to Polly," Pierre said, allowing her to march him to the back room. "She couldn't escape."

"Well, your story and Dillinger's conflict, and truthfully, I'd tend to believe him over you, because you're kind of a mean character. Now get in bed and don't come out until you're well. I don't want Rose catching your grunge."

"Arrgh!" He dropped his boots to the floor and rolled into the bed without further protest.

"Exactly," Auburn said, and closed the door.

She went back out to the family room, where Bradley and Dillinger were eating eggs and bacon and engaged in a discussion of the best ways to grow hay for cattle.

"Bradley, you don't know anything about farming or ranching," she said.

He shrugged. "I've always wanted a place in the country. I might as well learn something while I'm here."

Auburn sighed and wondered when the spaceship to her century would be boarding for takeoff.

"IF YOU EVER STAND in front of me again when someone points a gun at me, I *will* spank you," Dillinger said, coming into the kitchen to help her wash dishes.

Auburn smiled and said, "Promise?" which did not

make Dillinger's blood pressure go down one bit. The woman was driving him mad. Making love to her was all he could think about, to the point where he'd put a drop of laudanum in their companions' drinks last night. Hadn't someone once said that all was fair in love and war? Bradley and Pierre had gotten a good rest; he'd gotten a great night in Auburn's welcoming arms.

He was a happy man except for their two visitors, and wondering when Auburn was going to start talking about her little levitation act this morning when he'd kissed her. He feared that her time here was beginning to run out, though she hadn't seemed to realize it yet. The thought panicked him. He didn't know if he could stand the grief of losing another woman he loved.

He wondered if he'd have a choice, or if destiny was stacked against him, a bandit with more skill and cunning than he possessed.

"Hey," Bradley said, "where's the tree stand?"

Dillinger swore, resenting his rival's attempts to make himself at home.

"Uh-uh," Auburn said, "no cursing in front of the baby."

"Rose is asleep in her cradle in my room," Dillinger retorted. "And how do you expect me to feel when I've got your ex-fiancé in my house, cozying up to you?"

"I actually think he's cozying up to *you*," Auburn replied, snapping his behind with a dish towel. "Go help him. He's trying not to be a nuisance."

"Not very hard," Dillinger grumbled, and went to get the tree stand out of the shed.

Fifteen minutes later, he and Bradley had the tree in place. Auburn clapped her hands. "It's perfect!" she exclaimed, and Dillinger felt better, as if he'd given her something she really wanted.

He had to admit he'd started looking forward to the holiday. He'd been dreading it because Polly had loved Christmas, had loved putting pretty decorations on the tree. But somehow it felt right to have Auburn bringing Christmas to his lair, as she called it. He wondered if she would actually be here for Christmas, and felt edgy as he wished they were alone together.

Terror teased him as he contemplated her disappearing into the future.

"The star, please, Dillinger," Auburn said, and he took the star she'd made from some ribbon she'd found, and placed it atop the tree. "I made that just for you because you like stars so much," she said, giving him a gentle poke in the side.

Bradley shook his head and turned away from the tree to stoke the fire. Dillinger almost felt sorry for his rival, except that Bradley had proved himself to be unworthy of Auburn's love, and seemed to be accepting that he'd lost out on a good thing. Still, Dillinger didn't kiss Auburn in front of the man, even though he wanted to. Instead, he said, "I've got to go check some cattle."

"I thought you already did that," Auburn said.

"I was taking down a tree. I knew our two guests wouldn't follow me if they thought I was going to be out in the cold a long time with animals that are either surviving this storm or not." He put on his boots, lacing them tightly. "Want to come?" he asked Bradley, forcing himself to be sensitive to the other man's out-of-his-element feelings. "You can see a real ranching operation up close. If you can handle it in this weather, you'll know you were born to be a ranching man."

"Sure," Bradley said, delighted.

Auburn shook her head, got a few thick scarves from the closet and a big coat—of course Bradley was dressed for fashion, so he'd not stepped a foot outside yet—and Dillinger handed him an old pair of boots.

Bundled up against the cold, Bradley followed him out the door like a happy puppy. Dillinger turned to wave goodbye to Auburn, but she just shook her head again and blew him a kiss.

He went warm all over thinking about how good those lips could be to him. Old Man Winter and even forty degrees below zero couldn't steal the fire Auburn fanned inside him when she loved him. Just a smile from her filled him with delicious, soul-satisfying heat.

Please don't go, little one. Father Time, leave me with this one set of blessings, and I'll never ask for another thing as long as I live.

WITH PIERRE AND ROSE both asleep, and only an occasional hacking sound coming from Pierre's room, Auburn decided it was time to do some reconnaissance. She'd hidden Polly's earrings in Dillinger's room, so she went to locate them in the small matchbox she'd put them in, so Bradley or Pierre couldn't find them. Bradley wasn't the smoothest guy in this century, but he wasn't stupid, either, and she didn't want him figuring out the whole earring thing and going back with them. He'd sell them at Christie's to the highest bidder. She could just see it, *Magic Earrings for Sale— Serious Bids Only,* and shuddered. Although Bradley seemed as if he might be trying to change for the better, she knew greed would overcome.

Small and delicate, the earrings twinkled in the box, the dimness of the room doing nothing to diminish their luster. She could see them in Polly's ears, glittering at her lobes. How she must have treasured this gift from Dillinger.

Auburn didn't dare touch them, for fear of being swept away in time. When she'd be ready to leave Dillinger, Auburn didn't know; never, probably. Never, absolutely. Yet the time had to be close; something was warning her that she needed to be prepared for losing the only man she'd ever really loved.

"Please don't let the reason Bradley is here be because he's the man for me," Auburn whispered to the earrings. Then she closed the box, hiding it safely away again.

These were Dillinger's; no one should touch them but him, because no one else deserved to have his wife's things.

She heard pained snoring when she paused at Pierre's door, so she went on to the writing desk, kneeling down to peer at the hidden drawer underneath. "Antique furniture is so cool," she murmured, and pulled out Polly's journal.

But Auburn didn't dare peek inside. Her fingers trembled as she debated looking at just one page—but what if she opened the journal and something happened, such as her being sent into a time warp? Dillinger would be alone here with an embezzler, a mad trapper and a baby. After tracing the gold lettering with a gentle finger, Auburn turned the journal over to admire the firm binding.

She'd give anything to have another woman to talk to. At times like this she missed Cherie, although her sister wouldn't have any advice for the pickle Auburn was in right now.

The journal fell open in her hands. Auburn's jaw dropped. "I didn't do it, Polly," she said, quickly clapping the book shut. "I promised I wouldn't read anything private of yours. There's almost nothing so low as sneaking into a friend's diary."

She did consider Polly a friend. Even though she'd never met her, she had the strangest feeling that Polly was her one-woman cheering section. Auburn set the journal back into its hidden ledge.

It fell out onto the rag rug, open once more.

Auburn couldn't stand it any longer. She had to read Polly's words.

Dear Journal,
Every woman keeps secrets, even from her husband, her best friend. I love Dillinger with all my heart, but my heart is heavy with my secret. I always knew I couldn't bear him a child. I also knew how much he wanted children, but selfishly, I hoped our love could overcome the disappointment he would face eventually when he realized we would not have a child for him to call his own.

I didn't realize how this burden would affect me. Over time my love for him began to haunt me, because I knew what I had taken from him. Stolen, even.

That's what I did. I stole from the man I love, and what I took cannot be replaced.

There is a woman in a neighboring town who is ill. She can't take care of her baby, and she is desperate for someone to adopt her child. I'm going to do this, and I pray that doing one good thing for another soul will bless our marriage and our home with a child Dillinger can love.

Auburn gasped. "Rose!" Rose was the baby Polly was speaking of, she was certain, and her ghost had somehow gotten the baby to Dillinger's porch on that snowy night.

But Polly had died a year ago, and Rose had not yet been born. This was another child she watched over, and Polly was still with them, just in another place, a purgatory of her own guilt.

Prickles ran over Auburn's scalp. She lit a candle because the room was getting dark—the hour was growing late—and looked down at the page again, to reread Polly's journal entry.

But the words lifted off the page and dissolved in a shower of twinkling light.

Auburn slapped the journal shut, her heart racing. "Polly!" she breathed, hiding the journal safely away, not daring to read anything else. She picked up the self-portrait of the beautiful woman. "Polly, Dillinger loved you even though you didn't bear him children."

Polly smiled back at her.

"I don't know what to do," Auburn said, but she knew she'd been given the reason why baby Rose had appeared on Dillinger's doorstep that fateful night.

And Polly wanted her to make sure the baby stayed with him.

Auburn put the picture back on the desk.

She wished she had her computer so she could look up

Christmas River one more time. But she was positive she had searched thoroughly, and the town had not existed.

Something had happened to the community.

She had a funny feeling everything that happened in this house was destined to change the future of Christmas River. "I need a cup of Godiva hot cocoa so I can think," she said, and went to get Rose out of her cradle. "You don't realize you're an angel," she told the baby, kissing her forehead. The tiny girl flailed a fist, which brushed Auburn's chin lightly, and Auburn smiled, then froze.

She was once again floating off the ground. Her Uggs hovered at least four inches above the rug; she could freely kick her feet and not touch the floor. "Not the kind of party trick one wants to be known for, although it might be good for reaching the top shelf of my closet." She settled to the floor again, her feet solidly on the rag rug. Rose stared up at Auburn with calm eyes, and everything was as before.

But something was changing.

Auburn's body was getting ready to return to the century it belonged to.

She must not have long. Somehow she had to make Dillinger understand that Polly had intended for this baby to be his, for always.

So Polly could rest in peace.

Chapter Sixteen

Pierre's door opened and he staggered out into the hallway. He coughed, bending over with the effort.

"For heaven's sake, Pierre," Auburn said, "go back to your room. You're going to get baby Rose sick."

"I have to kill you," he said, his eyes bright with fever.

"You have no gun, because Dillinger took it," Auburn said calmly. "So your revenge will have to wait. Anyway, have you ever thought that maybe you should just try to remember the good things about your sister and not the things you imagine that were bad? Frankly, I haven't seen any indication that she was unhappy."

He leaned against a wall, shaking his head to clear it. "You don't understand."

She sighed, feeling almost invincible because she knew her physical body was starting to fade away. It was a little like being immortal; he could kill her in this century, she supposed, but she'd probably be halfway into her own by the time he got around to doing the deed.

Still, she felt she needed some backup.

"Excuse me," she said, sidling past him in the hall-way, "I need to tend to Rose's diaper."

She grabbed Polly's earrings from their hiding place, changed Rose, bundling her up securely. "Oh, I wish Dillinger were back! I'm afraid Pierre might make good his threat." She held the baby tight for a second, smelling her sweet scent. "I don't know if I'm supposed to take you or not, but I don't have a choice if Dillinger doesn't return soon. I can't leave you alone with that crazy man."

She went back out into the hallway, gave Pierre a shove that sent him stumbling.

"Hey!" he exclaimed.

"Don't breathe on the baby," she warned, holding Rose close and wishing again that Dillinger would come back. She wanted to hold him one last time, wanted to say goodbye, but if she'd learned anything here, it was that she had to rely on herself.

"Where's my gun?" Pierre demanded.

"I told you, Dillinger took it. But here's a little thought from my sister, Cherie, who insisted I join her for kickboxing lessons…" Auburn lodged a kick firmly in Pierre's gut.

He gasped, swore, staggered off to his room,

slammed the door. She could hear him coughing up a storm from the other side.

"Sorry, Polly," Auburn muttered. "He really needs a doctor."

She walked to the Christmas tree she'd trimmed with all the decorations she'd found in the attic, and wondered if she'd be here long enough to see all the pretty candles on it lit. She stared out into the snow, searching desperately for Bradley and Dillinger, hoping they hadn't gotten lodged in a snowdrift somewhere.

"They're big boys," she told Rose. "At least Dillinger is." She sighed, looked at the tree again with longing. "Hurry, Dillinger!" she cried out, feeling her hands go slightly numb. She wasn't surprised in the least to see them turn filmy, though she could still hold the baby. For that she could be momentarily thankful.

She went and sat in the rocker, pulled down one of Dillinger's leather-bound books, and held Rose close. "I never had a chance to read to him," she told the baby. "Your daddy likes to be read to. And I bet you will, too, one day."

And she clearly saw the picture that would never be: Dillinger holding Rose as he sat in front of the fireplace, this time with Auburn reading to him, all backlit by the beautiful Christmas tree.

It was her dream come true, her heart firmly in Christmas River with the man she adored. But as Pierre came lunging down the hall again, angry as a wounded bear, crazy with fever and maybe the snow madness, Auburn clutched Polly's earrings, held Rose tight, closed her eyes and let the future sweep her away.

DILLINGER WALKED INTO his house, saw his brother-in-law facedown on the rug in front of the fireplace. "Pierre, what the hell are you doing?"

He raised his head, his mouth slobbery and stuck with some fur from the rug. "Trying to kill your woman."

"My woman?" Dillinger glanced around. "Where's Auburn?"

"I don't know. She was here one second, and the next she was gone." Pierre laid his head back down.

"I think he's hallucinating," Bradley observed.

"We want him to think that," Dillinger said. "It's best that way." His heart was pounding, though, despite his brave words. Surely Pierre was only out of his head? Auburn wouldn't leave him or Rose, Dillinger was certain.

Bradley's eyes were huge. "I'm sure Auburn is around here somewhere."

Realization flooded him and Dillinger s heart went into a panicked overdrive. Every nerve, every inch of his soul screamed out.

She was gone!

He was going to die of a broken heart.

"She kicked me," Pierre said, his tone pitiful, "and I think she broke one of my ribs."

Dillinger smiled grimly. Auburn wouldn't have hurt anyone unless she'd felt threatened.

Pierre groaned. "My sister would never have kicked anyone. It's unseemly."

"You dope," Bradley said, "it's unseemly to try to kill a defenseless woman with a baby."

The baby! Dillinger had nearly forgotten Rose in his abject heartbreak that Auburn was gone. He was hoping she'd walk out of her room any minute, and they'd all laugh at Pierre's fever-induced hallucinations. But the house was eerily quiet, bereft of a baby's cries, laughter, or Auburn humming.

"Auburn! Rose!" he shouted, striding to the bedroom. She wasn't there. And she wouldn't have gone outdoors with the baby, not with it being about ten degrees outside.

His heart shattered, more painful than a gunshot wound.

It was three days before Christmas Eve. He should have known he couldn't escape the curse of Christmas.

He wanted to take the tree and toss it out the door into the snow. He hated Christmas and always would, forever and forever. This was the second time he'd lost a woman he loved in this cursed season, but this time he'd also lost a child.

Bradley peeked into the room. "I don't suppose she's here?"

Dillinger shook his head, unable to speak past the burning in his throat.

"Aw, man. That stinks, dude. I'm real sorry for you."

He and Bradley had had a long talk while they were out checking fences and cattle. Bradley had confessed that he was ashamed of what he'd done, had no intention of carrying through the terms of the loan. He'd also realized Auburn was a great person, but not necessarily the woman he wanted. All this realization had come to him after staying in Dillinger's house a few days.

"I didn't want to do the corporate thing all my life," Bradley had said, "and that's just part of the deal with the McGinnises. You can't see it in Auburn now, but she loves her Versace, her Vera Wang and her Vuitton. She calls them the three *V*s of bliss."

Dillinger didn't know what those were, but he figured Auburn knew what she liked, and that was okay with him as long as she moved him onto the Bliss List.

"It's expensive keeping up with a girl like that," Bradley had told him, and Dillinger felt sorry that Bradley didn't realize a man should be enough for a woman, and not feel any less because of his financial situation.

In the end, the two of them came to an agreement, and Dillinger decided Bradley was all right, he just needed a few years of seasoning in the country. With hard work he'd toughen up a bit and make a worthy human.

Pierre, he wasn't so certain about. He walked into the

living room, gave his brother-in-law a nudge with his boot. "Pierre, where's Rose?"

"Poof," Pierre said, waving one hand as he lay face-down on the rug. "Auburn disappeared, and she took the baby. Just a common thief, after all."

Bradley and Dillinger looked at each other.

Dillinger shook his head, the light dawning. He'd seen the signs; he'd known a change was coming.

I shouldn't have left her.

"There's one of those earrings," Bradley said, pointing.

Polly's earring lay on the rug. Dillinger picked it up and put it into his duster pocket.

Heartbroken, crushed with shock, he pulled Pierre up off the floor and dragged him to the guest room, gently placing him on the bed. "Do you want me to go for a doctor?"

"Did you go for one for my sister?"

"Yes, damn it, I did," Dillinger said, then sighed. "Don't be a madman, Pierre. I know you're grieving for her. Everyone loved Polly. The last person who wanted anything to happen to her, though, was me. She made my whole world a better place."

Pierre moaned. "You'll never make it if you try to get the doc for me."

"I'd give it my best shot."

His brother-in-law stared at him through fever-glazed eyes. "I'd settle for you wrapping my rib cage so I don't

scream when I cough. Your woman packs a helluva kick
with those ugly boots she wears."

Dillinger went to get some cloth, sorely tempted to
bind Pierre's mouth, as well as his ribs. But he figured
the man had been punished enough. He'd made his own
prison of hate, which was the worst way to live, as any
dead gunslinger's ghost could have told him.

"WHOA!" AUBURN LET OUT a squeak as she and the baby
landed on a nice, comfy sofa in the lobby of the Hilton
hotel. "Holy smokes! Are you all right, Rose?"

She was stunned the baby had made the journey; she
hadn't known if Rose would come back with her.

The child looked at her with gentle eyes, just as
she'd been looking at her a few moments ago in Dillinger's house in Christmas River. Rose didn't feel
cold; she was warm as toast, in fact. The only things
Auburn had been aware of was a *whoosh* and then
cold, and a subtle tearing as she was sucked through
time. But the baby didn't seem to mind their unexpected trip.

"Hey!"

A young, friendly desk clerk walked over to her. "I
remember you."

"You do?" Hadn't it been about nine days since
she'd left?

"Yep. You were dressed a little differently."

"Oh, yeah." Okay, so Polly's green dress wasn't fashionable, but Auburn was going to have it dry-cleaned and put away to show Rose one day.

"Your boyfriend stayed here for a couple of days, waiting on you to get back. And your parents paid for your room until the end of the month. We were supposed to make sure your car stayed safe, and keep your room just as it was. Your parents said they always believed you and Bradley—Mr. Jackson—would get back together once you had time to work everything out. At least that's what your mom told the manager."

Auburn blinked. "So all my stuff is still in my room?"

The desk clerk shrugged. "Everything. And your sweet little convertible is in the parking lot."

"Oh, my gosh! That's great news!" For once, Auburn didn't mind her parents meddling and trying to help out. "May I have a room key? I've misplaced mine. I think I left it in the room."

"Sure." The clerk smiled, and Auburn was reminded of herself at that age. The baby-faced young woman snapped her bubblegum and handed over a key card.

"This is wonderful," Auburn said, thanking her lucky stars. "Rose, sweetie," she said, going up the elevator, "we may not make it home by Christmas, but we will make it home. Together."

Maybe it wasn't as wonderful as spending Christmas with Dillinger would have been, but Auburn knew that her life had changed for the better, all because of the cowboy from Christmas Past.

She had no choice but to move forward.

For Rose's sake.

Chapter Seventeen

Auburn charged her cell phone, grabbed Pampers and baby wipes and hugged her Louis Vuitton bag. "I can't help it," she said. "You're beautiful!"

She knew she'd never again take for granted being able to buy luxury items.

She changed Rose, who seemed in quite good spirits for all she'd been through, even offering Auburn a tiny smile.

"Oh, they say when a baby smiles it's just gas, but I don't believe that for a second. I think you know you're the special one around here." She kissed the baby and picked her up. "I guess I'll never know if you were the magic or the earrings. And I feel terrible I left your daddy behind. I'm glad you came with me, though."

She tucked Rose in her cushy carrier. "I'm going to have to figure out how to get you a birth certificate and a passport. You and I can do some globe hopping and perfume launching now that our company is ours again, with Bradley out of the way. And we're going to develop a new line of baby friendly perfumes and lotions, all natural, totally biocompatible, because no one can appreciate what you babies had to go through before the days of easy baths and food on every corner and good medicine. We'll call it Baby Planet, and donate all proceeds to mothers with children they need help raising, in honor of your mom, who Polly wanted to help." Auburn kissed the infant on the nose. "You'll be a perfect spokesperson."

Everything would be perfect, except the fact that she'd never know what happened to Dillinger. To Bradley, either, for that matter, but that didn't seem to occupy her mind as much. "Shallow of me, I know," Auburn murmured, "but Bradley actually seemed happy in Christmas River. I suppose he'll always be the kind of guy who lands on his feet. But Dillinger…"

Dillinger had wanted her for herself, and she knew that was the difference between the two men in her mind. She loved him with all her heart and soul, every cell of her being, no matter the century. But Dillinger would want her to take good care of the baby Polly had given him.

She had to be strong.

"I'll wonder from time to time whatever happened to your yucky ol' uncle Pierre, too," Auburn told baby Rose, packing up their things. "I do hope he survived his bronchitis or pneumonia or whatever he caught from being a stalker."

But she would never know what had happened to any of the three men she'd left behind, and there was nothing to do but take Rose home to New York City.

AUBURN WAS THRILLED to be on the road. She drove like the wind for two and half days, determined to be home for Christmas. It was hard driving without her gun-slinger for company. The baby slept mostly, but Auburn wasn't in the least bit tired, an effect she chalked up to the time-traveling.

All she did on the long drive was think about Dil-linger.

It was too late for her to realize she was totally head-over-heels in love with the man. Impractical, since she'd never see him again. But she'd given him her heart will-ingly. "I just wish I'd told him I'd fallen in love with him." Every romantic tune on the radio made her eyes tear up.

Finally, the drive was over. Exhausted, Auburn walked in the front door of the penthouse, calling "Merry Christmas!" A smile lit her face when she heard answering squeals of joy; she was instantly enveloped by her sister's and mother's arms, her father patiently waiting his turn for a hug and a homesick kiss.

"And who is this angel?" Auburn's mother asked. Tall

and slender, Barbara McGinnis looked like a model in spite of her love of baking Christmas cookies.

"This is Rose," Auburn said, as her parents and Cherie cooed over the infant. "I'm adopting her."

Her father blinked. "Aubs, dear, do you need a baby? What does Bradley think about this?"

"Bradley and I are not together. And I think you have your company back now. We'll find other financing. He liked Rose, though, so he'd approve of me adopting her."

"What happened to the parents?" Cherie asked, her eyes sparkling as she looked at the baby. "Come to Aunt Cherie, honey," she said. "You just remember, any little thing you want, your auntie will make sure you get." She giggled and the baby grinned back at her.

"Rose's mother passed away, and her father is unable to take care of her." It was only a tiny fib; Dillinger loved to take care of Rose, but there was that matter of over a hundred years separating them.

"That's so sad," Cherie said. "But now we have our own little doll for Christmas. You sweet angel," she murmured against Rose's head, already smitten.

Barbara and Charles hugged Auburn again. "It's so good you're back," her mom whispered. Her dad was too choked up to say much. They just smiled at their daughters and the new arrival, looking like people who'd just been granted a miracle.

"Are you and Bradley all right, though, dear?"

Barbara asked as the five of them went to sit around the Christmas tree.

"Absolutely. By the end of our vacation together we'd come to the conclusion that we wanted very, very different things in life."

Barbara wiped her eyes and held out her arms. "Give me the baby, Cherie. You're hogging her."

Auburn smiled. It was just the reception she'd known Rose would receive. From orphaned to spoiled, Rose deserved a Christmas miracle.

"Can I see you in the kitchen, Auburn?" Cherie asked. "I need a little help mixing up some eggnog. Or cocoa."

"Maybe Christmas-tinis," their father suggested, trying to get the baby away from his wife so he could have a turn holding her. "And definitely a plate of cookies for Santa, please."

"Because Santa hasn't had enough today," Cherie said once they were in the kitchen. The sisters laughed, hugged each other again.

"It's great to be home," Auburn exclaimed. "You have *no* idea how much I've missed it."

"Go ahead, spill," Cherie said. "I can tell by the look on your face that you're wrapping everything up nice-nice for Mom and Dad, and sitting on the real story."

"I wouldn't know where to start."

"It involves a guy," Cherie prompted. "Did you and Bradley really finish off on good terms?"

"Yes. We weren't the same people we'd been before."

"You do seem different," Cherie mused. "More calm, maybe."

Auburn took out the cocoa, measuring it into cups. "I needed some time away." She was far from calm. Heartbreak had taken her over.

"And so you met a man…." Cherie reminded her.

"I did," she said, "but he's not available, so don't start getting too excited. He'll never be available." She felt bad about leaving Dillinger, and she hoped he'd forgiven her for doing so and taking his child.

"Ooh, not a married man!" Cherie cried. "You don't want to fall for the lure of the married man."

"Cherie!" She laughed in spite of her sadness. "I would never even look at a married man. No, Dillinger doesn't live anywhere where I could ever see him, so it's a nonstarter." The words were hard to speak. The realization she would never see him again tore at her.

"So you had a fling with a man you knew was geographically unavailable," Cherie said, "and yet our family has its own private and company jets."

She hadn't thought that far through what she was going to tell her sister; she had to tread carefully. "It's hard to maintain a long-distance relationship," she said with sadness, not able to tell her sister the real reason she could never see her cowboy again.

"Well," Cherie said, warming the milk for the cocoa,

"you probably needed time to get Bradley out of your system. I never did think he was the man for you."

"You didn't? You never said that." Auburn put some cookies on a platter and wondered why her sister hadn't mentioned her misgivings.

"You were determined to be perfect," Cherie told her. "I'm the younger sibling, so I'm allowed to learn from your mistakes. One thing I've learned is not to be so darn perfect all the time." She grinned. "Don't let Mom and Dad try to push you into a marriage at the ripe old age of twenty-seven if you don't want to be married."

"Oh," Auburn said, "they'll focus on you now. Twenty-five is plenty marriageable."

"Yes," Cherie said with a smile, "but I'm not afraid to mess up the script. Part of our problem is that we're always worried about what people will think of us because we're the face of McGinnis Perfumes. I'll be the black sheep who brings excitement and a little scandal to the brand."

Auburn shook her head ruefully. She couldn't share her secret, of course, but she'd had enough excitement and scandal to last her for a lifetime—or at least a few years, anyway. What would her parents have thought if she'd brought home a gunslinger? She smiled wistfully as she thought about how wonderful Dillinger was to her. And to Rose.

She was going to miss that big, hot-blooded, hunky cowboy.

Like crazy.

She pushed the terrible heartache away and went to find Rose.

DILLINGER SLOWLY NURSED Pierre back to health, and taught Bradley how to be a rancher and how to survive in the coldest of winter conditions. He missed Auburn, but he knew she was wherever she had to be.

Their relationship had never been part of destiny, he'd decided. Every once in a while he'd pull Polly's earring from his pocket, wonder if Auburn had taken the other one. Maybe it would show up one day. He didn't think the earring was the key to her returning to her century; he'd seen her body begin to grow filmy and then reappear, and she hadn't had the earrings with her then.

She'd never been meant to be part of his era, that was all. Maybe his role had always been to take Rose to Auburn, a woman who would love her and care for her, and make certain she grew up to be a fine young lady.

Auburn was the perfect woman to do all that. He smiled when he remembered that he'd thought she was a woman of loose morals when he'd first met her. Over time, he'd realized her true character: she was a hard worker and a positive spirit.

She and Polly would have been such good friends, had they lived in the same time.

Now he had two roommates instead of a woman. Life was funny that way.

"Hey," Bradley yelled from the kitchen, "who wants venison chili for dinner?"

Pierre looked up from stoking the fire. He couldn't do a lot because of his ribs, but he did try to help out, in return for Dillinger letting him rest up in his house until the hard freeze passed. There was little light in the sky, even during the day, and he had no sleigh even if he were well enough to travel, which he wasn't.

Dillinger only slightly regretted chopping up Pierre's sleigh. He'd been mad that day, angry, tired of being hounded by the man. Taking it out on the sleigh wasn't a very productive use of his energy, but it had made great firewood. And he was making a better sleigh for Pierre as an apology, and hopefully a mending of their relationship.

"I'll take some chili," Pierre said, "and I'll do the washing up, since you did the cooking."

It was amazing how those two were making a great effort to get along. They were changing, Dillinger realized, trying to become better people. Stronger men. Men who didn't hold a grudge, didn't hold people hostage for financial reasons or revenge.

Maybe he'd become a stronger man, too, thanks to Auburn. "I'd like some chili, too," Dillinger said. "You've become quite the cook in the past few days."

Even Christmas had been a tasty affair, though he still preferred Auburn's cooking, especially her Christmas turkey soup. He'd loved everything she'd prepared, everything she'd done for him. Bradley had made game hens stuffed with rice and spices, surrounded by vegetables. Three men spending Christmas together hadn't seemed all that festive, but on the other hand, he hadn't been alone, and Dillinger had been grateful for that.

The Christmas miracle was that they'd all sat and talked in front of the fire, and put all the bad history behind them. Bradley didn't feel as if Dillinger had tried to steal his woman anymore, and said he realized Auburn hadn't been his true love, after all. Pierre said he knew he shouldn't have tried to kill a man who'd loved his sister, and was glad that the Christmas spirit had finally cured him of his grief.

Dillinger said he didn't give a fig about either of them, but since they were in his house, they might as well share a cup of wine with him. They'd laughed, not taking offense, and enjoyed the holiday with forgiving hearts.

Except Dillinger, who'd quietly nursed a broken heart.

"I guess I won't travel back," Bradley said as they sat eating their chili. "I don't seem to be getting any particular call to return, and I can't say I'm all that unhappy. I like it here." He glanced around Dillinger's comfortable house. "I like not living for the bottom line. I want to build a place just like this one."

Dillinger grunted. "I'd sell it to you."

Pierre and Bradley stared at him over raised spoons. "You would?" Bradley asked.

He nodded. "I don't want to be here. It's time for me to move somewhere else. Maybe California."

Pierre blinked, his handlebar mustache drooping. "And your cattle?"

Dillinger put his spoon down, realizing exactly what he was going to do. "I'm selling it all, lock, stock and barrel. The whole thing. I want to start over, somewhere far away from here."

Pierre and Bradley looked at each other. "Want to go into business?" Bradley asked. "I'm still a bit of a greenhorn, but between the two of us, we could probably make a good go of it."

"That's true," Pierre said. "Unless you think you'll disappear one day. I can't run this place by myself. I'm not the loner that Dillinger is."

Dillinger thought he would give his soul to never be lonely again.

"I think I have to want to disappear," Bradley said, sending a sheepish look toward Dillinger. "I really wanted to find Auburn before, and I had the earring she'd left behind in the hotel room. I really don't want to find her now, and even if I did, I don't have a talisman to make me travel."

"We never knew if the earring was what made it all happen," Dillinger mused.

"And I think you're all cracked," Pierre said, "but your secret's safe with me because no one would ever believe me, anyway."

That was true. There were days when Dillinger wondered if he'd only imagined holding tiny Rose and loving Auburn.

But then he'd think about how happy they'd made him, and he knew he hadn't imagined a thing.

He just wanted it all back.

He laid the earring on the table. They all stared at it as it shone in the bright candlelight.

"It's yours if you want it," he told Bradley. "You really don't know how hard these winters are. If this earring is a ticket to the future, you're the one who should have it."

"I'm staying in Christmas River. Pierre can show me everything I need to know," Bradley answered. "I feel like I was meant to be here. Maybe there's even a woman here for me. In the spring, perhaps Pierre will take me to town, introduce me around." Bradley stuck out a hand for Dillinger to shake. "Pierre and I will take good care of everything."

Dillinger nodded and shook Bradley's hand. "You'll find a new sleigh in the barn, Pierre, better than your last one."

"I'll take that, but I don't want the earring, either," Pierre said. "My sister adored them. She would have wanted you to do with them as you wish. But I do not need a keepsake of her." He smiled, sadly. "I have my good memories, and that's all I need now."

"Try it, Dillinger," Bradley urged. "What have you got to lose?"

Pierre nodded. "God hates a coward," he said simply.

Dillinger stared at the golden earring with the tiny bells. He didn't really believe the earring was his magic ticket. He knew there were magic carpets and genies in bottles in books, but this was real life, and a practical man understood that harsh reality was the way of the world. "I don't believe in it," he said. "My destiny was to take Rose to a good mother. I was only the bridge."

"You don't know that for certain," Bradley insisted.

"It's not good to live off old memories," Pierre added. "At least give it a try."

Dillinger glanced at the fireplace where he'd sat many times in front of a roaring blaze. He looked at his favorite books on the ledge, and the two rocking chairs nearby. He gazed at the Christmas tree Auburn had decorated with such love, such hope. And then he looked at Polly's self-portrait in the tiny frame. She seemed to smile at him.

Polly had always encouraged him. But he was afraid to dream that he and Auburn were meant to be together.

"I don't know how to believe in anything but hard work," Dillinger said.

"How did it happen before?" Pierre asked. "Were you holding it? What did you do when you went to Auburn last time?"

"I was thinking about Polly, and I laid her earring on the writing desk," Dillinger said slowly. His fingers closed tightly over the earring. "And then I heard a cry on the wind, a baby's cry, as impossible as that seemed, so I opened the door and I—"

Sudden wind snuffed out the two candles on the table.

The room was enveloped in darkness.

"I've got it," Bradley said, lighting the candle nearest him.

"I'll light this one." Pierre struck a match and held it to the candle at the other end. Bradley looked at Pierre, and Pierre looked at Bradley. Then they looked at the empty chair, and the fire in the hearth that had blown out with a great puff of white smoke, and the evening stars shining bright as diamonds through the window.

Bradley said, "You know, one day they're going to put a man on the moon, just that easily."

"You have quite the imagination, my friend, which is good for long winters," Pierre replied. And then they laughed and went back to eating the delicious chili, not worried at all about the future.

Chapter Eighteen

The two-branched candelabra at the dinner table suddenly blew out with an emphatic *poof!* A faint tinkle of bells sounded, and then there was a crash in the McGinnis dining room.

"Goodness!" Barbara exclaimed.

"Someone must have opened a couple of doors," Cherie suggested.

"Or maybe a gust came down the chimney," Charles said.

They all glanced at the stone fireplace in the living room. A fire burned merrily behind an elaborate scrolled grating. The Christmas tree, bright with all its silver and gold trimmings, twinkled with tiny white lights.

"We should check the fireplace," Barbara said. "I'd hate for a spark to jump out on the rug."

The entire family got up from the table to go do so.

"I don't see anything," Auburn said, but a chill ran over her arms.

"I don't, either," Cherie retorted.

Rose lay in a huge white playpen swathed with lacy white bumper pads and cushiony quilts. She was asleep, contentedly sucking on her thumb, her little bottom raised in the air as she slept. Tiny booted feet poked out from underneath a white blanket.

"She doesn't seem to have been bothered by whatever that gust was," Barbara said with a fond smile.

The chills stayed with Auburn, intensifying. Surely she wasn't about to time travel! She wanted to stay here with her family. Below the penthouse was her own apartments, and below that, Cherie's, while McGinnis Perfumes had the fourth floor down for its marble-lined offices. Auburn wanted to stay where she knew Rose would have a good life. She needed time to nurse her broken heart. She needed time to learn how to become a good mother.

Yet the chills gripped her. She reached into the pocket of her white evening pants, feeling for the earring, realized it was gone.

She wasn't going to travel. Maybe she'd picked up a small space-bug from all the jaunting across the centuries.

"Are you all right, Auburn?" Cherie asked. "You look like you've seen a ghost."

"I'm fine," she said, and then they all stopped.

Listened.

Heard it again.

A baby's cry.

"It's coming from outside," Auburn said, wondering how anyone could have gotten up to their floor without them buzzing a visitor through.

"Be careful," Charles said, "we really should have Security check outside first."

Auburn slowly opened the front door—and then smiled.

Dillinger lay on the doormat as if he'd been gunned down by a gunslinger. But he was smiling, his eyes lighting up when he saw Auburn. "I missed the chimney," he said. "I was hoping to do a Saint Nick-style appearance."

She helped him up, threw her arms around his neck. "We have a roaring fire in the fireplace," she whispered against his cheek.

"Good thing I missed, then," he said against her hair.

They could have held each other for an eternity.

Behind them Cherie said, "Oh, wow, it's Jesse James," and Auburn smiled. Dillinger did look like something out of an Old West postcard, sinfully handsome enough to turn any female's head in the big city.

"Come in and meet the family," Auburn invited, and he removed his cowboy hat. "Mom, Dad, Cherie, this is Dillinger Kent."

"Welcome," Charles told him. "Something tells me

the little Rosebud in there will be awfully glad to see you when she awakens from her nap."

Barbara McGinnis beamed at Dillinger. "Welcome to the family," she said. "Come in and make yourself at home. I hope you're planning on staying for Christmas dinner."

Dillinger's face was solemn as he gazed into Auburn's eyes. "Bradley says he believes we had to want to travel. Wanting to is the key."

"Oh, we don't listen to Bradley anymore," Cherie said.

Dillinger held Auburn's eyes with his, knowing the answer he had to have. "You weren't running from me?"

"God, no!" Auburn threw her arms around him again. "I'm in love with you, Dillinger Kent. If anything, I would have run *to* you. But never away." She softly touched his face. "You're not angry that I took Rose?"

He kissed her, a light, intimate brush with his lips that conveyed his emotions. "I trust you with her life."

Joy enveloped Auburn, replacing all the worry, all the doubt she'd held inside.

Dillinger nodded at the McGinnises. "I'm staying as long as Auburn will have me. I love her."

Auburn's heart glowed inside her. The chills were erased by a warmth she couldn't explain, warmth she knew would never go away as long as she was by Dillinger's side. She put her hand in his. "Then you'll be staying forever," she said softly, and led him into the living room so he could hold his daughter in his arms.

He picked up his child, and baby and father grinned at each other, perfectly delighted, a matched pair. Then Dillinger reached for Auburn, pulling her into his embrace, and she knew just how long their time together was meant to last.

They were a family—forever.

Epilogue

"Now this is a fantasy come true," Auburn said, gazing at Dillinger. Over his protests, she'd talked him into wearing a pair of black trunks, but he'd given up complaining once he saw other men dressed in swim trunks. Auburn appreciated the swimwear on her husband—she would never get tired of looking at his strong, sexy body. Under the bright Hawaiian sun, smelling the ocean breezes and soaking up warmth, she'd spent a week watching her cowboy turn dark brown and more gorgeous by the minute.

"I'm still not used to everyone seeing you in this garment you call a bathing suit," Dillinger said, nibbling on her neck as he leaned over her on the chaise longue. "But the weather here is so nice that I almost feel sorry for Pierre and Bradley."

"Don't be. They got the ending they wanted, and it was a happy one," Auburn said, enjoying him caressing her back as she lay on her stomach. "Smell the coconut oil and be glad to eat the island cooking. It's better than mine." She smiled as he poured more suntan oil onto her back, taking his time about rubbing it into her skin.

"Are you sure Rose is all right at your parents'?" Dillinger asked for the tenth time that week.

"You know, you can use that new iPhone to text Mom and Dad and ask." Auburn smiled. "Rose is fine. I think she's a spoiled princess, and when we get home, she'll probably be insufferable."

Barbara, Charles and Cherie had jumped at the chance to have little Rose to themselves for two weeks while Dillinger and Auburn honeymooned. Dillinger had been eager to fly on a jet—*real* traveling, he called it—and so after their wedding in New York City, surrounded by friends and family, Auburn had gifted him with a surprise honeymoon to Hawaii.

He'd been utterly fascinated by the whole experience, a kid in a candy store.

And when they'd landed in the beach paradise, he'd been awestruck.

"Do you think you'll like working for my father?" Auburn turned her cowboy over, began to rub suntan oil into his muscled skin, enjoying the task at hand, taking her time. It was making it really hard to wait to get him back to the room after supper, but she couldn't bear to drag him out of the sun just yet. For

a man who'd hated Decembers, Dillinger was beginning to fall for the enchantment of Christmas and the
whole winter season. He enjoyed lying in the sun, and
Auburn loved looking at him. "Hey, bronze god," she
said, "you don't have to work for Dad if you don't
want to. Although he says you're just what the company needs."

Dillinger grinned slowly and sensuously. Her heart
pounded as she recognized the promise in his smile.
"Don't worry. Bottles of perfume are much easier to
handle than a thousand head of cattle. I'm excited to
travel around the world on one of those big planes and
sell beautiful women things to make them smell pretty."

She lightly smacked his arm, laughing at his teasing
words. "I still think you'd be happier living on a ranch,"
she said, but Dillinger shook his head.

"Let me get tired of living in the picturebook of New
York City first," he told her. "I'm enjoying the feeling
of never being alone. I look out the windows, down at
the sidewalks, and I see people. I'm enjoying sushi res-
taurants and Starbucks. It's your world, and I like it."

She smiled contentedly. They touched hands, curled
their fingers together and lay on their chaises, enjoying
the sun. "You know, I've searched for Christmas River
on the computer a hundred times, but I can't ever get it
to come up. Yet I know it was there," Auburn said.

He shook his head. "Don't ask me what happened to

Christmas River. I can't even figure out if it was the earrings or Rose that brought us together."

"Polly," Auburn said. "I always thought it was Polly who did that."

He kissed Auburn's hand, nibbled her fingertips. "I found her picture in the pocket of my duster, but I know for certain I didn't take it off the writing desk."

Auburn smiled. "I'm glad. Rose will want to see it one day." She thought about how to make her confession, and then said, "Dillinger, I never told you that Polly had a journal."

"In the writing desk."

"Yes."

He grinned. "Who do you think built the desk and the secret hiding place?"

She laughed. "Polly wrote that she loved you. You knew all along you could prove your innocence!"

He shrugged his rock-hard shoulders. "I didn't care to. I answer to no one but myself." He sent Auburn another devilish grin. "And maybe now…Rose."

She wouldn't tell him Polly's secret, Auburn decided. Some things were best left in the past, preserved in a time capsule, never to be opened. She arched a brow. "Speaking of answering for things…do you remember when I told you I wear a little device inside that keeps me from getting pregnant?"

"Yes, and I don't like the thought of it," he said,

scowling. "It's not a part of modern medicine I wish to be employed in our home."

She flashed her own devilish smile. "I have a doctor's appointment when we get back to have it—"

"Good," he interrupted, kissing her long and slowly. "Rose needs brothers and sisters. We should work on that as soon as possible."

Auburn giggled. "We'll practice often."

"We may practice now."

"I love you, Dillinger Kent." When he kissed her hand, pressing her palm to his lips, she shivered, knowing exactly what those lips were capable of.

"Mrs. Kent, woman of my heart and of my dreams," Dillinger murmured, "can I show you to your room for some before-dinner refreshment?"

She nodded. "That would make me a happy wife, Mr. Kent. And later tonight, I plan on reading you a very romantic bedtime story."

He helped her up. Then he took her by the hand and they walked together up the beach, under skies that were just beginning to soften with sunset.

Some places, like Christmas River, were heaven in different points in time. She and Dillinger would always hold that special place in their hearts. And being together was certainly heaven on earth, for all the many blessed and wonderful Christmases to come.

* * * * *

*Celebrate 60 years of pure reading pleasure
with Harlequin®!
Just in time for the holidays,
Silhouette Special Edition® is proud to present
New York Times bestselling author
Kathleen Eagle's
ONE COWBOY, ONE CHRISTMAS*

Rodeo rider Zach Beaudry was a travelin' man—
until he broke down in middle-of-nowhere South
Dakota during a deep freeze. That's when an angel
came to his rescue....

"Don't die on me. Come on, Zel. You know how much I love you, girl. You're all I've got. Don't do this to me here. Not *now*."

But Zelda had quit on him, and Zach Beaudry had no one to blame but himself. He'd taken his sweet time hitting the road, and then miscalculated a shortcut. For all he knew he was a hundred miles from gas. But even if they were sitting next to a pump, the ten dollars he had in his pocket wouldn't get him out of South Dakota, which was not where he wanted to be right now. Not even his beloved pickup truck, Zelda, could get him much of anywhere on fumes. He was sitting out in the cold in the middle of nowhere. And getting colder.

He shifted the pickup into Neutral and pulled hard on the steering wheel, using the downhill slope to get her off the blacktop and into the roadside grass, where she shuddered to a standstill. He stroked the padded dash. "You'll be safe here."

But Zach would not. It was getting dark, and it was already too damn cold for his cowboy ass. Zach's battered body was a barometer, and he was feeling South Dakota, big time. He'd have given his right arm to be climbing into a hotel hot tub instead of a brutal blast of north wind. The right was his free arm anyway. Damn thing had lost altitude, touched some part of the bull and caused him a scoreless ride last time out.

It wasn't scoring him a ride this night, either. A carload of teenagers whizzed by, topping off the insult by laying on the horn as they passed him. It was at least twenty minutes before another vehicle came along. He stepped out and waved both arms this time, damn near getting himself killed. Whatever happened to *do unto others?* In places like this, decent people didn't leave each other stranded in the cold.

His face was feeling stiff, and he figured he'd better start walking before his toes went numb. He struck out for a distant yard light, the only sign of human habitation in sight. He couldn't tell how distant, but he knew he'd be hurting by the time he got there, and he was counting on some kindly old man to be answering the door. No shame among the lame.

It wasn't like Zach was fresh off the operating table—it had been a few months since his last round of repairs—but he hadn't given himself enough time. He'd lopped a couple of weeks off the near end of the doc's estimated recovery time, rigged up a brace, done some heavy-duty taping and climbed onto another bull. Hung in there for five seconds—four seconds past feeling the pop in his hip and three seconds short of the buzzer.

He could still feel the pain shooting down his leg with every step. Only this time he had to pick the damn thing up, swing it forward and drop it down again on his own.

Pride be damned, he just hoped *somebody* would be answering the door at the end of the road. The light in the front window was a good sign.

The four steps to the covered porch might as well have been four hundred, and he was looking to climb them with a lead weight chained to his left leg. His eyes were just as screwed up as his hip. Big black spots danced around with tiny red flashers, and he couldn't tell what was real and what wasn't. He stumbled over some shrubbery, steadied himself on the porch railing and peered between vertical slats.

There in the front window stood a spruce tree with a silver star affixed to the top. Zach was pretty sure the red sparks were all in his head, but the white lights twinkling by the hundreds throughout the huge tree, those were real. He wasn't too sure about the woman hanging the shiny balls. Most of her hair was caught up on her head and fastened in a curly clump, but the light captured by the escaped bits crowned her with a golden halo. Her face was a soft shadow, her body a willowy silhouette beneath a long white gown. If this was where the mind ran off to when cold started shutting down the rest of the body, then Zach's final worldly thought was, *This ain't such a bad way to go.*

If she would just turn to the window, he could die looking into the eyes of a Christmas angel.

* * * * *

Could this woman from Zach's past
get the lonesome cowboy to come in
from the cold...for good?
Look for
ONE COWBOY, ONE CHRISTMAS
by Kathleen Eagle
Available December 2009
from Silhouette Special Edition®

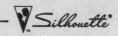

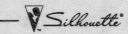
Silhouette®

SPECIAL EDITION

**FROM *NEW YORK TIMES* AND *USA TODAY*
BESTSELLING AUTHOR**

KATHLEEN EAGLE

ONE COWBOY,
One Christmas

When bull rider Zach Beaudry appeared
out of thin air on Ann Drexler's ranch,
she thought she was seeing a ghost of
Christmas past. And though Zach had
no memory of their night of passion years
ago, they were about to share a future
he would never forget.

*Available December 2009
wherever books are sold.*

SSE65493

HARLEQUIN
Ambassadors

Want to share your passion for reading Harlequin® Books?

Become a Harlequin Ambassador!

Harlequin Ambassadors are a group of passionate and well-connected readers who are willing to share their joy of reading Harlequin® books with family and friends.

You'll be sent all the tools you need to spark great conversation, including free books!

All we ask is that you share the romance with your friends and family!

You'll also be invited to have a say in new book ideas and exchange opinions with women just like you!

To see if you qualify* to be a Harlequin Ambassador, please visit
www.HarlequinAmbassadors.com.

*Please note that not everyone who applies to be a Harlequin Ambassador will qualify. For more information please visit www.HarlequinAmbassadors.com.

Thank you for your participation.

BAP09BPA

REQUEST YOUR FREE BOOKS!
2 FREE NOVELS PLUS 2 FREE GIFTS!

HARLEQUIN®

American ★ Romance®

Love, Home & Happiness!

YES! Please send me 2 FREE Harlequin® American Romance® novels and my 2 FREE gifts (gifts are worth about $10). After receiving them, if I don't wish to receive any more books, I can return the shipping statement marked "cancel." If I don't cancel, I will receive 4 brand-new novels every month and be billed just $4.24 per book in the U.S. or $4.99 per book in Canada.* That's a savings of close to 15% off the cover price! It's quite a bargain! Shipping and handling is just 50¢ per book. I understand that accepting the 2 free books and gifts places me under no obligation to buy anything. I can always return a shipment and cancel at any time. Even if I never buy another book from Harlequin, the two free books and gifts are mine to keep forever.

154 HDN E4DS 354 HDN E4D4

Name _____ (PLEASE PRINT) _____

Address _____ Apt. # _____

City _____ State/Prov. _____ Zip/Postal Code _____

Signature (if under 18, a parent or guardian must sign) _____

Mail to the **Harlequin Reader Service:**
IN U.S.A.: P.O. Box 1867, Buffalo, NY 14240-1867
IN CANADA: P.O. Box 609, Fort Erie, Ontario L2A 5X3

Not valid to current subscribers of Harlequin® American Romance® books.

Want to try two free books from another line?
Call 1-800-873-8635 or visit www.morefreebooks.com.

* Terms and prices subject to change without notice. Prices do not include applicable taxes. N.Y. residents add applicable sales tax. Canadian residents will be charged applicable provincial taxes and GST. Offer not valid in Quebec. This offer is limited to one order per household. All orders subject to approval. Credit or debit balances in a customer's account(s) may be offset by any other outstanding balance owed by or to the customer. Please allow 4 to 6 weeks for delivery. Offer available while quantities last.

Your Privacy: Harlequin is committed to protecting your privacy. Our Privacy Policy is available online at www.eHarlequin.com or upon request from the Reader Service. From time to time we make our lists of customers available to reputable third parties who may have a product or service of interest to you. If you would prefer we not share your name and address, please check here. ☐

HAR09R2

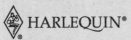

HARLEQUIN®

A Cowboy Christmas
MARIN THOMAS

2 stories in 1!

The holidays are a rough time for widower
Logan Taylor and single dad Fletcher McFadden—
neither hunky cowboy has been lucky in love.
But Christmas is the season of miracles! Logan
meets his match in "A Christmas Baby," while
Fletcher gets a second chance at love in "Marry
Me, Cowboy." This year both cowboys are on
Santa's Nice list!

*Available December
wherever books are sold.*

"LOVE, HOME & HAPPINESS"

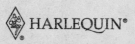

COMING NEXT MONTH

Available December 8, 2009

#1285 THE WRANGLER by Pamela Britton
Men Made in America
For as long as she can remember, Samantha Davies has dreamed of Montana's legendary Baer Mountain mustangs. She has to see for herself if there's truth behind the legend...before she loses her sight forever. And nothing, not even the devil-handsome wrangler Clint McAlister—who has every reason to distrust Samantha's intentions—is going to stand in her way. Because time is running out.

#1286 A MOMMY FOR CHRISTMAS by Cathy Gillen Thacker
The Lone Star Dads Club
With four preschoolers between them, neighbors and single parents Travis Carson and Holly Baxter don't know what they'd do without each other. And they don't want to find out! Everything changes when Travis's little girls ask Santa for a mommy for Christmas. Their entire Texas town gets in on the hunt for an available mom...who happens to live right next door.

#1287 HER CHRISTMAS WISH by Cindi Myers
The only thing Alina Allinova wants for Christmas is to stay in the U.S.—oh, and Eric Sepulveda. They're having a fairy-tale romance, yet the possibility of sharing a happily-ever-after seems far away, with her visa expiring soon. Still, her fingers are crossed that come Christmas morning she'll get her wish and find him under her tree!

#1288 A COWBOY CHRISTMAS by Marin Thomas
2 stories in 1!
The holidays are a rough time for widower Logan Taylor and single dad Fletcher McFadden—neither hunky cowboy has been lucky in love. But Christmas *is* the season of miracles! Logan meets his match in "A Christmas Baby," while Fletcher gets a second chance at love in "Marry Me, Cowboy." This year both cowboys are on Santa's Nice list!

www.eHarlequin.com